I0729979

GOINGS-ON
on
GARDENIA LANE

Goings-On on Gardenia Lane

d.j. posner

Copyrighted Material

Goings-On on Gardenia Lane

Copyright © 2025 by D.J. Posner. All Rights Reserved.

All rights reserved. No part of this book may be reproduced or transmitted in any form or by any means, electronic or mechanical, including photocopying, recording, or by any information-storage and -retrieval system, without permission in writing from the copyright owner.

This book is a work of fiction. Names, characters, places, and incidents either are the product of the author's imagination or are used fictitiously, and any resemblance to any actual persons, living or dead, events, or locales is entirely coincidental.

For permission requests or to order additional copies, contact:

D.J. Posner
www.djposner.com
posner.easton@gmail.com

ISBNs:
978-1-7369399-7-0 (hardcover)
978-1-7369399-6-3 (softcover)
978-1-7369399-8-7 (eBook)

Library of Congress Control Number: 2025906061

First Edition: 2025

Printed in the United States of America

Cover and Interior design: 1106 Design

This book is dedicated to the friends
of Shell Road Beach

Prologue

Born the only child of two theatrical parents, I was given the lyrical name of "Delilah Paris" at birth. As an adult, I became a writer and adopted the simple nom de plume "Paris," which is how I am known to the inhabitants of St. Michael's Key. This twist of anonymity has afforded me a cloak to my past, to days long gone, which, given my need for privacy, served my purpose well.

St. Michael's Key, a charming barrier isle located off the shores of Sarasota, Florida, was the place I had decided to make my new home. The first showing my real-estate agent had for me was on Gardenia Lane, a sweet enclave of renovated bungalows nestled on the north end of the Key. I was fortunate to have found such a glorious habitat, and its quiet locale suited me to a "t."

Darlene D'Angelico was my neighbor in the next bungalow down the lane, so I was a witness to her life's comings and goings. Yes, I knew her and her legendary antics, and I didn't care for the woman; she was just too dangerous. Therefore, I wasn't surprised to hear the news of her ghastly murder. I had heard the sirens heading down-island at dawn and wondered what had happened. When the news trucks raced by with their big satellite feeds on top, one right after the other, everyone looking for the scoop, I knew it was something big. The last time there was that much excitement on St. Michael's Key was when a World War II munitions pack washed up on Little Beach, containing the explosive SOE-supplied Nobel 808, the same dynamite used in one of the assassination attempts on Adolf Hitler.

I followed my hunch and walked up to the best vantage point on the west side of the island. At Little Beach, you could see the crescent stretch of beach all the way down to where the Key gave way to the inlet running between it and Castle Key, thereby separating the two isles by a mere half mile. It was said that, in very low tide, you could wade between the two.

I reached the wooden bench on Little Beach and looked across the Gulf to a bevy of red flashing lights. The Gulf's undulating currents in these parts form shallow shoals. These shoals have shifted over the years, as the waters ebb and then retreat, all the while guiding ancient as well as modern-day mariners through the Pass and into the Bay of Sarasota. The sandbar emerging off the point of down-island Samson Beach and stretching out for a mile or so arises in the midsection to form a sturdy and reliable dune covered in exquisite shells and sea life. In that regard, the locals had named it Sand Dollar Island, accessible only by boat.

The flurry of Sheriff and Coast Guard activity on the water, coupled with the flashing lights on Samson Beach, afforded me a clue that someone was either hurt or dead. I was thinking dead from drowning, but I was dead wrong. As it turned out, it was a homicide. Found was the partially clad and mutilated body of none other than Darlene D'Angelico. Hours later, when I learned of the murder, I didn't give pause. What I did was sit down and begin my own list of suspects, for most everyone on this sleepy little island had something against that woman. There were just too many people who longed for her demise.

Chapter 1

Paris

A CURIOUS LOOK AT THE MOVEMENTS of my fellow islander Darlene and my snooping into the D'Angelico family history was fascinating. They were not known to be personable people. They kept to themselves. Their affiliation with the New York mob was widely scandalized, but nary a fact had ever surfaced to prove it. They were a careful sort. Yup, from every appearance, the D'Angelicos were cautious, even circumspect, that is, until Darlene became of age. The new breed of D'Angelicos of her generation stretched all earlier molds, and Darlene was the boldest of the brood. Darlene was fast. She was cunning like a fox, with eyes that squinted in considering her every move, and you always knew that *in that move*, she'd be on the run.

Darlene was once married to Cal Calisto, one of the more respected lieutenants in the Brooklyn-based Lucchese family. Cal's death was widely rumored to be the result of his being set to become a federal witness. His name was known to be next on the hit list. When I read this rumor, I wasn't sure what to believe. With Cal dearly departed, Darlene was cast aside by the family. Deep in debt from legal fees and a lavish lifestyle, she used her masterful craftiness to reinvent herself, and that is when she surfaced down on Florida's Suncoast to the island of St. Michael's Key in a bungalow on Gardenia Lane.

Desperation does funny things to a woman. Most men live lives of quiet desperation. Not so for a woman, especially a woman with an agenda. If the image of temptress comes to mind, well . . . you get the picture. Darlene was always looking to resolve her mounting debts. She was wild within that complexity, emphatically self-absorbed, and she would not hesitate in the least to insert herself into the lives of others. Inevitably, when other, unsuspecting people were linked to Darlene, something sinister would follow.

One of her hangers-on was the brilliant land developer Nico Stefanos. Blinded by her beauty and known to easily spiral out of control, Nico clung to Darlene like it was his job. Too many times, Nico followed her down into her world of wantonness and debauchery. Years passed before Nico ever realized that his only sin was losing his heart to a wounded tigress who could never be tamed. Like many before him, Nico was an emotional support dog for Darlene, enabling her to broadcast her foul sputum into the world.

It was Nico I met first. I had settled on Gardenia Lane after being transplanted from the landlocked Colorado town where I'd spent my young-adult years. Strange as it was, Nico had lived on the front range of the Rockies, several canyons over from where I called home. I guess it was this connection that first bonded the two of us.

Darlene surfaced in this quasi-friendship much later in the process. She had sniffed around a lot in the beginning, never considering me a threat. Her attempts at entangling me into female neighborly rapport failed instantly and miserably. Try as I might, I just could not find common ground with the woman. Always one to hold suspicion up front like a breastplate, I would walk away from any encounter, leaving her to plot her next tackle.

Nico, on the other hand, possessed an innate intelligence, a worldly swagger, and informed opinions. We had a lot in common. I never, however, could figure out how the two of them ever got together. The politics of romance make for odd bedfellows—*very* odd.

Darlene used her beauty to great advantage. She was physically enhanced to attract the weak at heart. Her long-tinted tresses indecently revealed breasts, and long, deeply tanned legs made her conquests, male or female, stack up like a deck of cards. She was one woman whose company was something I dismissed as disposable. My refusal to become attached only intensified her full-court press. I kept to myself, as I had learned to do, mostly for self-preservation, but really to remain in the safety of my anonymity.

Chapter 2

Paris

THE MORNING DARLENE'S BODY WAS DISCOVERED, I returned to the house after spending more than an hour seated on Little Beach, like an interloper to the unfolding scene in the distance. As soon as I entered through the front door, the phone was ringing piercingly. At this early-morning hour, I knew that it would not be a telemarketer on the other end of the line. I dove for the phone and was relieved to see my neighbor, Suzy Atwater, pop up on my call screen. She was out of breath, and I felt my heart beating faster to keep up with her patter.

Suzy was an odd mix of sophistication and sensibility. The vast experience that she gained by living all over the world had rounded out her perspective. I always found myself walking away from our deep conversations feeling fully advised and able to put my finger on an answer to any question. Suzy's face always wore a suggestion of a smile that lightened her expression. And it was in this illumination that her true compassion was cast. I was lucky, in that Suzy adopted me as if I were a local, letting my transplanted persona melt away to nothing. The sort of blanket acceptance she provided me made for a cryptonymous role, and it kept my assumed public image in the forefront of inquisitive minds.

Suzy's dialogue poured out of her mouth like spilled milk. As had I, she had been monitoring the covert island activity, her feed coming from the police-band radio that she always had on in the background. She confirmed the discovery of the body of a blond female of the approximate age of 45 who was beautifully adorned in expensive jewelry. Suzy's breathless recounting of these findings left me producing more body oils than average and with my hair standing on end. There was nothing in her frenetic narrative that led either of us to a conclusion about the identity of the decedent. Suzy's summation aligned with mine that this apparent death was by drowning, either accidental or otherwise. As Suzy monitored the police feed, she halted suddenly, her calm turning to a shriek.

"Oh, my gawd, oh, my gawd, honey, the body was found to be partially nude and mangled. This is no ordinary death; it must be a murder. Who on Earth could the victim be? How on Earth can this be happening here on St. Michael's Key? Oh, my gawd!"

As the particulars continued to filter through the radio scanner, I attenuated my thoughts before responding.

"Suzy, I am getting an unsettled feeling here. These new details sure fit the description of our neighbor, Darlene." And as I spoke the words, I looked down the lane toward Darlene's abode, now eerily quiet and devoid of activity. It was as if, within the stillness of the property, there was enough probability that my assumption was correct. I swallowed hard and bid farewell to Suzy. She promised an update as more facts came to light.

Later that day, the confirmation came in, identifying the body as none other than that of Darlene D'Angelico. Knowing it was just a matter of time before the detectives showed up on Gardenia Lane to begin their investigation, I sat down at my computer and began an earnest search into the recent or past activities of the late Ms. D'Angelico. It amazes me what one can garner from Google. It was important to me, in more ways than one, to stay informed as the fact-finding probe of this death played out.

As evening fell, Gardenia Lane was crawling with every gumshoe on the local force. The death of this doll was boiling over into headline news. Every resident on the lane was on notice. Nothing brings people together better than a common enemy.

A maelstrom consumed our normally "neighborly" hamlet, and we all shuddered with unease at the mystery of this whodunit. Being Darlene's next-door neighbor, I was the first to be interviewed. My one-word responses led to silence and sidelong glances from the detectives and, I guess, put me on the list of persons of interest. How could I respond otherwise?

The woman was a crushing bore at best and one to whom I couldn't cotton to save my hide. While her pretentious vexation was an annoyance to me, it certainly wasn't like the thorn in the flesh felt by many other persons who would delight in seeing Darlene wiped from the face of the island. Darlene's adversaries were just too many to count.

At the end of the day, the only thought I was left with was the adage *The enemy of my enemy is my friend.*

Chapter 3

Paris

A KNOCK ON THE FRONT DOOR disrupted my concentration. I was busy writing an article for *Cosmopolitan* magazine titled "17 Hair Tricks for Dealing with Humidity." I wasn't under a deadline, but I was still entrenched in the mechanics, and any infringement renders me sidetracked. I pushed away from the desk, all the while stretching and groaning.

I opened the door to the flushed face of Detective Francisco Cruz, one of the officers who'd made the initial point of contact with me the night before.

I said, "Hello, Detective Cruz. What can I do for you?"

Cruz wasted no time in small talk. "Could we talk inside, Ms. Paris?"

Shaking the cobwebs from my mind, I took a step out onto the porch, saying "It's a lovely evening. Let's talk out here." I was clearly adhering to the old axiom *Never give consent without a warrant.*

I settled myself into one of the porch Adirondacks, while Cruz, I guess, decided standing would keep him at an advantage. I waited for the detective to speak his piece.

Cruz, leaning casually against the porch rail, began his litany of the whys and wherefores on the finding of Darlene's body, complete with narration and summary points.

Strange, I thought as he droned on. Have any conclusions been drawn already? This bird-dog investigator was aligning some kind of framework by surmising the probable cause of death and affixing that theory to his suspicions regarding members of our neighborhood *barrio*. Wow.

Gardenia Lane was a treasure trove of characters, to say the least. And I kept most of them within my inner circle. Yet, there was much I believed that I didn't know about the cast of eccentric souls who shared my landscape. I should talk: I carried my *own* hidden mystery, carefully concealed under a veil of secrecy. Years of maneuvering within this *modus operandi* kept my persona secure, my background unchallenged.

Chapter 4

Paris

As is immanent in the tropics, the rain began at 4 o'clock the next day. I was battened down in my writing studio when I heard the car pull up outside. The short lanes and side streets on the north end of the island accounted for little traffic, as the waters of the Gulf can come across on every westerly boundary. I got up and stretched as I looked out the window. It was Bobbi St. John, my neighbor from across the alley. She came skittering up the walk, a tangerine umbrella quelling the sheet of rain that was falling as I swung open the door.

"Hey, Bobbi girl," I called as she swept into the room shaking like a canine.

"Not fit for man nor beast!" she replied.

I hadn't seen Bobbi since the news had broken, and I was certain that was the reason she'd stopped in, despite the torrential rain falling. I forged ahead right into the subject:

"So, whataya make of all the goings-on?" I offered, not letting on that I knew a thing or two about it, all the while gauging her body language for a reaction. Her response was more of a snappy comeback.

"I'd just gotten back from Miami this afternoon when I ran into Suzy at the market, and she spilled the beans. How dreadful that something like this could happen on our sleepy little Key. Whatever happened to the 'Take-your-dog-to-work nation' and not locking your doors at night? I mean, murder just changes the whole picture—it changes everything."

I listened carefully as Bobbi made known her fears and angst. Bobbi was one competent woman—fit, qualified, and well-versed. In her former life, she'd been a model and actress who got her start after her stint as a centerfold and a reign as Playmate of the Year. She was still recognized around town from starring in TV's *Supergirl,* in which she appeared for several years in the late '90s. Even in her advanced years, Bobbi remained quite the looker. Those years had been kind to her, and, although she was single, she was never at a loss for male companionship. Men flocked to her like blind dogs in a meat market. Her genuine and forthright manner made her easy to love.

After her conversation subsided, I made us a cup of tea. Thinking ahead, I also poured a two-finger snifter of Remy Martin for both of us. The hour was close enough to 5 o'clock, and besides, I thought the situation warranted it. We settled back into the deep cushions of my down sofa and began to dish. I shared the details I had learned so far and explained the finer points of the two encounters I'd had with Detective Cruz. By the time we hammered through the questions of the *whys and wherefores*, the rain had subsided, and I began my routine of moving around the kitchen.

Bobbi wasn't interested in food, so she took the opportunity to gather herself up and move toward the door. She explained that she still had things to unpack and put away before the week started. I was sorry to see her go, as her energy had filled my space and quelled my wandering mind.

The ladies of the north end of the island had become like a pseudo-family. Strange as it seemed, when I came to settle on St. Michael's Key under my shroud of secrecy, a ready-made consortium awaited me. Suzy Atwater was the first to draw me in. I had arrived with pocketsful of memorized stories that made up a colorful background, one that carefully concealed the facts and circumstances of my landing here. My age lent itself well to the persona I'd created, and, so far, I'd been successful in maintaining the camouflage. If there was ever a "delve" into any nuance of my story, my reply was always, *"Can you keep a secret? Good—so can I!"*

Settling into the social structure that these women companions had already established wasn't difficult, but it did take finesse on my part. Being a writer, I instinctively knew that natural, female-inquisitive tendencies could easily give way to snooping and peering if my credentials were not ironclad.

So, as it was, and keeping that tidbit in mind, I formed and moderated the monthly Fun Friday Night Book Club to cluster these gals around me and forge a deep commitment to *listening*—not with their mouths running but *hearing* and *learning*.

That is what contributed to some of my greatest performances. I parlayed the quiet and introspective persona I had adopted into an easily approachable public image. So successful was this portrayal that my island neighbors chose to make me one of their own, and that suited me just fine.

Chapter 5

Detective Francisco Cruz had just come from a twelve-hour shift when he caught the D'Angelico case. *How opportune,* he thought, as he'd long had an interest in the furtive, backstairs activities associated with Darlene. She was well-known by law enforcement, always on the fringe of lawless activity, mostly perpetuated by nonsensical, frenetic domestic disagreements with her flavor-of-the-week.

Cruz had been assigned to the elite Homicide Division a few years back, after having moved through the ranks and proving his working understanding of the law and its enforcement. The split-second decisions he made and his success in apprehending countless thieves, thugs, and routine collar arrests resulted in notice by the Detective Bureau. It was his investigative experience in the areas of organized crime and narcotics dealing that the name of D'Angelico had first appeared on his radar.

Cruz's first efforts were to inspect Darlene's residence again. The morning of the discovery, Cruz and the two uniformed officers accompanying him on the scene left Sand Dollar Island, while the investigator for the medical examiner's office was concluding his findings. The three cops headed for Darlene's residence on Gardenia Lane. During the initial visit, other than the carport being empty, the house and grounds yielded little in the way of clues. Everything appeared in order—nothing out of place. Cruz's reaction on that morning was that Darlene had clearly made herself up for an evening on the town. Her makeup was out on a dressing table, a discarded Lycra T-shirt was lying on the bed, and the closet door was ajar. A pair of thong sandals was next to the bed, and the closet floor looked as if it were missing one pair of heels. Everything was neat as a pin. This initial, perfunctory visit would be followed up the next day.

As the next morning bore down, Cruz made his second visit to the residence, intending to conduct a more thorough investigation and begin filling in the many blanks. By doing so, he hoped to add some puzzle pieces on the mostly empty Discovery Board back at the station house.

Cruz scribbled some notes in his book and left the station house shortly after eleven the next morning. He headed away from downtown traffic, working his way over the north causeway to St. Michael's Key. Gardenia Lane was located on the north end of the island, so he swung into Darlene's residence about 11:20 a.m. All in all, Detective Cruz felt he had a thorough, wide-angle view of Darlene's movements leading up to her departure from the house the night she died. Now, he just had to narrow them down to a bird's-eye view.

The preceding afternoon, he had pulled the registration tag from the Motor Vehicle Administration and placed a BOLO out on her vehicle. On this day, he exited his sedan and proceeded with caution, giving further regard to the exterior surroundings. He bagged a lone cigarette butt with a gold tip that he discovered out near the border of the Lane, but other than that, nothing seemed out of the ordinary.

As he continued to move about the residence taking copious photographs, he noted the trace scent of perfume still lingering in the foyer. His thoughts automatically went to the conclusion that this doll had been dressed for a date. He proceeded into the kitchen and opened the refrigerator. Inside was just the obvious empty vastness of a single person's contents—an open bottle of white wine, a carry-out container from L'il Ting's in the Village, and bottles of spring water. He then moved to the living room, where he saw the single wine glass sitting on the coffee table, empty and with lipstick on the rim. He switched on the TV—the last channel watched had been CNN. *Hmmm . . . this dame follows politics*, he thought.

Gazing out of the windows of the lushly furnished lanai overlooking the bayou canal and carrying out into the azure-gray penumbra of the Gulf of Mexico, he pondered as to where Darlene might have been traveling that fateful night. Was she meeting a clandestine lover? Was she meeting a first-time blind date? A business associate she hoped to bed and then perhaps swindle?

Cruz moved smoothly around the room, hoping to garner a stronger sense of her movements. In the kitchen, he rifled through the mail but found nothing of interest. He did, however, extract two credit-card statements from the stack and neatly stashed them into his breast pocket. From the near-empty trash can, he retrieved the formally addressed outer envelope from what appeared to be an invitation. The embossed return address was from the Bird Bay Yacht Club. *That's interesting*, Cruz thought. *I wonder what event the Yacht Club was hosting and when that event had been scheduled.* Unable to discern any further detail from the discarded envelope, he tucked it into his pocket for a detailed follow-up.

Moving back into Darlene's bedroom and dressing area, he again noted the closet and the obvious empty dress hanger and missing pair of stilettos. The dresser drawer to her lingerie chest was askew, so he drew the drawer out and peered inside. The drawer contained neatly arranged sets of lacy garments and, notably, one empty space. *It's becoming more and more obvious that this dame had been headed out for a rendezvous of sorts—that much is certain,* he thought.

Cruz's initial interviews with the neighbors on Gardenia Lane did not result in any much-sought data. The opportunity to interview Bobbi St. John had not presented itself yet; Cruz planned to stop by there on his way out. He'd been successful in reaching out to that cute writer next door. She was an interesting creature, a loner—and one he intended to follow up with as his investigation progressed.

Suzy Atwater, who lived the farthest from Darlene, in the first bungalow on the lane, was a very intelligent—yet risky—sort of person. Cruz had done some research on her and found that she was a well-known archaeologist. Her CV showed she had followed in the footsteps of scholar Alana Cordy-Collins, studied Peruvian pre-history, and then continued her studies under Cordy's cousin, a chief archaeologist for the Commonwealth of Hawaii, in the study of Polynesian cultures.

The PhD Suzy had earned from UCLA was a buried background fact. However, the building block that made this little *Suzy* most interesting was that every person or vehicle coming onto Gardenia Lane would have to pass by her door. Suzy, it seemed, may know way more than she lets on.

Chapter 6

Paris

I SYSTEMATICALLY APPROACHED the following morning with my routine cup of tea and a beachfront half-hour of yoga to free my mind. My devotion to yoga had begun many years ago in Colorado. I had become a zealous believer in its physical and spiritual benefits. It was the one discipline that helped keep me centered.

The sun was streaming in through the windows, and in its radiance, I relaxed my frenzied mind. I sat down to my archaic word processor and began to do more research on Darlene's life patterns. My study was less investigative in structure and more in keeping with the *listening and learning* temperament I had adopted. To me, the more I could garner about her movement, the broader my understanding of her character and temperament would become.

Although it was a long time ago—and by now resolved and settled into the deep recesses of my mind—the tale of how I became to be confined to solitary life—estranged from all I knew before—was a sordid one. The loneliness that had pervaded my heart all these years was ever-present, and no amount of discipline, friendship, or other camaraderie could ever squelch it.

Harry Burroughs was the reason why. Harry was my partner, my lover, and my dearest friend. He was gone, and I could never seem to get past the fact that his death had landed me in the quagmire that had become my life.

I had met Harry Burroughs in a particular season of my life, when I was fresh and youthful. I was an investigative reporter for *The Denver Post*, working on a story about crime in the Mile-High City. That first meeting became an unrelenting constant in my world. From day one, we became bonded and existed in each other's world just as a well-worn accessory would enhance its model. I loved Harry Burroughs. His maturity—15 years my senior—didn't deter my capricious heart. Even his difficult job did not scare away my idealistic, quixotic fancy.

Harry was a cop. In the bloody world of Denver's street-gang scene, Harry was a committed detective, attached to the coveted Vice Squad and involved in activities surrounding the rampant and expanding cartel-fueled drug trafficking that pervaded the Rocky Mountain State's largest city. It was a convoluted case that Harry was chasing that took his life and changed mine forever in the process. And in that loss, I remained as I do today, heartsick and alone.

Chapter 7

Detective Cruz sauntered into the precinct and heard, "Hey, Cruz. I heard you caught the D'Angelico case." The voice was a shout-out from Jeremy Brosnan, an eager beaver and newly minted detective 3rd class. Cruz responded with a grunt and proceeded to log onto his computer screen without further comment.

The notes and observations from his assessment of Darlene's residence were fresh in his mind, and he wanted to add them to the Discovery Board. The documentation of the scene had produced little on which to build a motive . . . so far. He had hoped that the information gathered from canvassing her residence a second time and interviewing neighbors and known associates would provide some clarity as to who would want Ms. D'Angelico dead. Plainly put, and from every account, there was hardly a soul who cared if she was alive or dead. The woman was not well-liked by anyone.

That opinion seemed to spread from the island grocery-store clerk to the next-door neighbor to the landscape company that handled her property. And, if the woman had any friends, well . . . they had remained anonymous so far.

As Cruz's fingers ran swiftly across the keyboard, he accessed some systems and programs which dredged up some of Darlene's past. Even though there were multiple domestic disturbances and misdemeanors, he saw nothing he could use that provided any solid lead.

Once the information he discovered was merged into the timeline and the data he found from his search through the NCIC (National Crime Information Center) neatly organized, he proceeded to bounce a well-worn basketball while he sat staring at the ceiling. Basketball was Cruz's passion, and when he wasn't hunting America's most wanted, he was glued to a game of hoops.

As Cruz gathered his thoughts, his mind drifted to the former boyfriend of Darlene's, Nico Stefanos. Even though the relationship between the beauty and the mogul gave every appearance of being *kaput*, Cruz's intuitive power led him to conceptualizing, which usually further led him in the direction of a tip.

One of the facts he was able to uncover thus far was that, several years ago, Darlene had, more or less, swindled Nico Stefanos out of the deeds to several undeveloped properties on the island. The documents in the court case were voluminous and resulted in Darlene coming out blazingly victorious, due to Nico's *unclean hands*. And, while Nico Stefanos could well afford losses in most any market, his legendary hold on his Greek roots and traditions prevented him from allowing any woman to trod on his livelihood, let alone his manhood.

Yes, Cruz fully intended to spend some time with this gentleman as soon as Stefanos returned to the States from his summer holiday on his native Mykonos. Cruz looked forward into the calendar and determined that Stefanos' return was just weeks away. His mind then wandered, and, in his contemplation, he speculated if word of Darlene's demise had created a "wave over the pond" that could reach Nico's ear. Next, he wondered, *If this was the case, what was Nico's reaction to the news?*

Chapter 8

Mykonos, Greece

The isle of Mykonos was alive and with fervor. The seaport was lined with ferries bringing in tourists from the mainland. Nico Stefanos was holding court in the *agora* down by the harbor. Surrounded by a cluster of old Greek men playing *bocce*, Nico was in a seemingly deep discussion when his phone alerted him to an incoming text message. As he turned away from his conversation to attend to the message, his demeanor changed dramatically.

Gus Papadopulos, Nico's boyhood friend, noticed the change and immediately returned to Nico's side just as Nico lowered the phone to the table, his face white with shock. Gus said, "For the love of God, Nico, what's happened?" Nico's shoulders drooped as he picked up the phone and held the text message up to his friend's face.

A gasp emitted from Gus's lips as he turned his full attention back to Nico.

Darlene's demise had spread across the world and found its way to, perhaps, the only person who held any semblance of love for the woman.

The look of despondency on Nico's face was enough to prompt Gus to hustle them both up and head for a dark, cool place where they could seek quiet and a stiff beverage to quell the shock.

Once inside Porta Bar Mykonos, the lilting sounds of a *bouzouki* playing did little to soothe Nico's agitation. The two gentlemen settled into a booth in the corner while Gus signaled the waiter for two *ouzos*. The conversation was slow to start, but, once he was engaged, words flowed out of Nico's mouth in a torrent.

"I just spoke to her. We were trying to find common ground. She wanted to make amends, but I wasn't sure I could trust her again after the lawsuit that she filed against me. She said we weren't done with each other and that we still had things to talk about. How could this happen, and who could have done such a thing? I have never been able to get that woman out of my head; she had a hold on me that was gripping."

The two men sat in the tavern for more than an hour before Nico said he needed to head up the hill and see his parents. He was thinking that he should be making his way back to the States and cutting his summer vacation short. Would there be a funeral? Would there be an investigation, and if there was, who was on their list of suspects?

Certainly, the Darlene he had followed over the years since their introduction was artfully snaky, and her scheming, it seemed, always held her in disfavor with most souls. That is the way it is with self-serving, conniving people; they strew a path of destruction until the day comes when that destruction does an about-face and takes them down.

Chapter 9

CRUZ ARRIVED AT THE AUTOPSY FACILITY CENTER located on the campus of Sarasota Memorial Hospital. He reached the coroner's office around ten the next morning. He wanted a chance to meet with Dr. Alice Bullock, Sarasota County's Chief Medical Examiner.

Upon his arrival, there was some ancillary activity going on that took precedence over his meeting. Apparently, parents of a recently deceased nineteen-year-old had arrived to identify the body of their son, dead from an overdose. Cruz sat quietly waiting and allowed the space around him to be filled with grace.

The loss of a child deeply affected him—it was never an easy thing to witness the sadness from those left behind after a senseless death. To be an observer of this kind of scene was a sharp reminder that life is too short to take the kind of chances that accompanied street-drug consumption, because the deadly additive of fentanyl could always be laced into any substance.

Once Dr. Bullock cleared her office, Cruz stepped in.

"Say, Alice, I'm on the D'Angelico case; have you made any headway in your exam?"

Dr. Bullock, a pretty, petite Afro-American gal, smiled at Cruz while she reached for her binder on the case.

"I have taken some preliminary photographs to open the file, but I haven't eviscerated the corpse as of yet. I may get to it this afternoon. Why don't we go into the morgue and see what we have to work with?"

As Cruz rose from his seat to follow this diminutive figure down the grim, dark hallway leading to the refrigerated shelves where bodies are held, he couldn't help but wonder what would attract a woman to the study of pathology.

Dr. Bullock rolled out the shelf holding Darlene's corpse from its labeled chamber and pulled back the sheet. Cruz was not deterred by the condition of the body, noting that some were post-mortem changes, and some were a result of the method of death.

Without the doctor having had the chance to perform her examination, Cruz was not allowed to touch the body. Policy prohibited that until such time as the coroner could move the body through the exam, document the findings, and write her conclusions.

Observations, however, were most helpful at this stage. So, Cruz pulled out his notebook and made some notes as to what he saw. In a short while, the list became long as he scribbled, documenting a large contusion at the rear of the skull, some bruising around the collarbone, two broken fingernails, a partially ripped earlobe, and a huge bruise on the left thigh. There was no sign of animal or insect activity, and there was little decomposition, both indicating that her death was recent.

Cruz nodded to Dr. Bullock, so she slid the drawer closed and glanced at her clipboard.

"I should be able to get into this for you by this afternoon and finish up by the end of the week. Would you like me to call you when my report is written?"

Cruz told her he would and turned to leave, but as he did, he spun back around and asked, "Dr. Bullock, so far, I don't have much to go on, what with the body being found up on the Sand Dollar Island atoll. I've somewhat developed an outline from both the scene and the decedent's residence, therefore, any anomalies you might ascertain from your investigation would be most helpful."

Bullock responded, "Well, Detective, you don't know me well, but I do love a good mystery, so I will do my best!"

And with that being said, the two headed out of the ice-cold room and proceeded up the hall, walking almost in unison, matters of life and death preoccupying them both.

Chapter 10

Paris

SUZY ATWATER WAS OUT IN HER YARD tending to her staghorn fern as I rode by her house. It was not unusual for Suzy to be outdoors. As an archaeologist, she had lived all over the world and was involved in digs, enduring the most stifling heat while wrestling with sandy, arid conditions. In contrast, puttering around in her backyard in southwest Florida's late-summer heat was purely refreshing, if one is into that kind of thing.

I pedaled my bike past Suzy on my way down-island for my morning cup of tea, which I took to the shoreline of the Gulf each morning to stabilize my psyche, a communion I took seriously and never missed, rain or shine.

Strangely, the vantage point that I usually chose to complete my morning ritual was the same bench on Little Beach where I'd first gotten wind of the macabre goings-on. But today, I chose the shore of Samson Beach, which was directly in front of the atoll where Darlene's body had been found. I sat pondering for a bit longer than my normal *Zen* routine. While sitting there, I felt deeply unsettled by this recent, lurid event on the sleepy little key I now called home.

My curiosity was so piqued that it started to draw me back to my former investigative-reporter mindset, a persona I had kept tightly locked away. Here in the present, the character I played was that of a gal from out west who had relocated after being dumped by her longtime lover, who had fallen in love with someone much younger.

In this façade of a life, I portrayed myself not as a reporter but as a bookish, introspective writer of popular magazine articles and the like. Ever cautious, I decided to keep my former life concealed. Therefore, I would merely put out some covert feelers to my neighbors and local shop owners in the Village concerning Darlene's murder.

Someone, somewhere had seen or knew something. Either they didn't realize that any knowledge they had regarding the murder could prove useful, or they were keeping mute so as not to be involved. That's the way it is with an investigation; one must dig through a lot of muck before unearthing a clue.

Thinking about unearthing, I decided I would start with Suzy Atwater. She'd been trained in unearthing things, and, maybe, just maybe, from her vantage point at the end of the lane, she may know or have witnessed something of consequence. I hopped back on my bike and started to pedal back up-island, and by the time I reached Suzy's bungalow, it had begun to rain.

Suzy was no longer out in her yard as I rounded the corner, the light rain obviously a deterrent. I decided that, after I'd stashed my bike, checked my emails, and taken a quick shower, I would call Suzy and see if she would like to join me this evening down at Claudio's for a wood-fired pizza and a glass of Chianti. Hey, when a gal wants to "dish" on a topic, what better way to do so than over a great meal?!

A phone call to Suzy confirmed her interest in joining me. *Delightful*, I thought. *I enjoy Suzy's company, and she would be my best bet in developing a timeline of Darlene's recent movements.* I wrote out a list of questions and memorized them so I could slip them into the conversation naturally. Since Suzy held a social-science doctoral degree, she was less educated in the *psychology* of human nature and would likely suspect little if my fact-gathering expedition was presented casually.

I swung by Suzy's corner of the lane, into her crushed-shelled driveway, and gave a little toot of the horn. I had dropped the top on my red convertible, the fancy car just another prop in my scheme to remain undiscovered. Certainly, a girl newspaper reporter wouldn't own such a vehicle, but a gal from a well-to-do family transplanted from out west would . . . so. Suzy came sauntering out, wearing a smile, and hopped into the passenger seat. She said,

"Look at us two chicks! I really like riding around with you. It always makes me feel young again."

"Suzy," I laughed, "forget the numbers. You know you are only as old as your subjective age. You've been dealing with relics for so long, I dare say you have adopted the idea of being a mummy yourself!"

We both laughed at the thought as I accelerated down Beach Road, with our hair flying behind us.

Chapter 11

Paris

Suzy and I were warmly greeted by Claudio himself, complete with the traditional European two-cheek kiss, and then escorted to a comfortable booth along the back wall. *Great vantage point for people-watching*, I thought. Once settled, Suzy ordered a glass of Cabernet, and I stuck with an Italian Chianti, because, after all . . . *when in Rome!* Once the beverages had arrived and we'd ordered our favorite pizza, featuring Claudio's homemade sausage and roasted garlic, we toasted each other, and I got down to business.

Keeping the mood light and breezy, I opened our discussion with the topic at hand. I began my inquisitive probe by sharing snippets of conversation that I'd had with Detective

Cruz. Suzy, the type of listener who was more focused on what she was going to say next, blurted out,

"Oh—me, too. He stopped by my house yesterday afternoon. Said he had returned to Darlene's bungalow to accumulate what evidence he could and wanted to have a chat with me to see if I could shed any light on Darlene's recent movements."

Suzy stopped long enough to take a breath and then spewed on with her tale.

"Well, Cruz . . . you know he's known by his last name, like you are . . . well, he opened up a can of worms with me. I told him all about the run-in I'd had with her down at Morton's Village Beach Market the morning before Darlene was found dead. I was in the back, by the deli, looking at the beach hats hung on a rack. I wanted to replace the one I had been using when I garden, as it was no longer doing the job."

Once Suzy filled her lungs with a breath again, she continued her diatribe.

"Well, don't you know, here comes Darlene, dressed to the nines. She leans over and says, 'Suzy, you're too old for a straw hat like that—leave those for the 20-year-olds.' I mean that's so . . . I don't know . . . curt! *20-year-olds*, indeed. At least I don't go around at age 45 with my breasts hanging out on display for all to admire. And imagine—at a little beach market, she's dressed in a short white mini-skirt and high-heeled sandals—and draped in jewelry at nine in the morning. That woman thinks she's ultra-European, but what she really is, is ridiculous."

I had to laugh at Suzy's animated gestures as she told her tale, but I nodded in wholehearted agreement when she said the word "curt"! That woman, Darlene, was anything but likable to most anyone she encountered.

The conversation continued as we lingered over our meal, and I was ingesting copious mental notes on Suzy's chatter. She mentioned the landscaper gossiping to her about Darlene just last week. Suzy also filled me in on some gossip about the subject of Nico Stefanos and his expected return for the funeral.

Claudio came to our table at the end of the meal with a decanter of Limoncello and two cordial flutes.

"Belle signore, il mio regalo per voi," he announced in his silken native Italian accent.

A gift, indeed! Suzy and I gushed and thanked him profusely as we drew him into a brief conversation about Darlene. I mean, dames will be dames . . . we *dish!* Well, that action added some more insight into yet another aspect of Darlene's rash persona.

Claudio, anxious to share his prowess, recalled an encounter he'd had with our dead neighbor a month prior. Apparently, Darlene, "being Darlene," had made some quasi-suggestive sexual comments to him in hopes that he might bite, with an invitation to a date. He was laughing at her audacious and reckless attempts at flirtation.

"I knew one day," Claudio said, *"un giorno,* one day, she'd fool with fire and get herself burned!"

I guess he was right about that! And he was spot-on about her being careless, too—as cheeky as that dame was, one day it was all bound to catch up with her.

Chapter 12

Nico arrived on Air France Flight 5922 into SRQ Sarasota International airport, accompanied by his pal Gus. The two had been inseparable since Nico had received the news. Their connecting flight through Paris-Orly had them landing in Sarasota at ten at night and starving. Once they'd retrieved their luggage, they headed downtown to see what they could find open. It was Friday, and Main Street was still awake with activity.

The driver who had picked them up pulled into a space in front of the Gillespie Grill Restaurant. Before the two men exited the town car, they arranged with the driver to deliver their bags to Nico's nearby condominium building and handsomely paid the driver with a wad of cash. Nico quickly put a call out to the building's doorman to alert him of the arrangement. After all, being a penthouse owner does have its advantages!

The two gents entered the dimly lit dining room and slid into a booth. The cute waitress sidled over and turned on some charm after seeing two good-looking, deeply tanned, and well-dressed fellows take a seat in her station. Once they had ordered and sufficiently flirted back with the waitress, she took her leave, and the boys began to make some plans for the days ahead.

Darlene's funeral was on Monday. Nico wanted to visit the tailor at Tweeds to have his black suit pressed and altered if necessary. Gus suggested that they also hire a boat to take them to Sand Dollar Island, just so Nico could pay his respects. Although it was not Darlene's actual gravesite, Gus thought Nico would want to lean on his Greek traditions, perhaps by erecting a shell-and-stone marker and delivering an epitaph in Darlene's honor. After all, the funeral would not be the place to rue his loss of the one woman of whom he could never completely rid his system. A private, personal ceremony of sorts was definitely in order.

Nico slept fitfully that night. Gus was comfortably ensconced on the futon in Nico's office and sleeping deeply. When Nico arose and picked up his keys from the bureau, he was able to slip out quietly and unnoticed. Nico headed to *C'est la Vie!*, a neighborhood French bistro to pick up some breakfast treats for him and Gus. There was a line out the door when he arrived. At the end of the line, Nico recognized a realtor friend of his, Sue Brown. He knew Sue was with Michael Saunders & Company and worked out of their main offices right around the corner. He walked back in her direction and greeted his old friend.

"Hello, Sue. Seems we are both hungry early birds."

"Why—Nico Stefanos. Hi, there. You look great. Wow—what a great tan. Are you just back from your summer retreat in Greece?" she replied.

Nico quipped back, "Yes, indeed. As you know, I go every year to visit with my parents. As one knows, you can take a Greek boy away from his home, but he will always return to recharge!"

The friendly banter with Sue continued without a lull as the line inched forward. Once inside, the two friends headed in separate directions, bidding each other farewell. Nico thought to himself that word had certainly gotten around town about Darlene's death and wondered why Sue had never mentioned a thing about it. Nico had met Sue years ago when she represented both the seller and him, as buyer, in a real-estate transaction. He was deep in a relationship with Darlene at the time, so Sue was certainly familiar with their longtime involvement. *Strange,* he thought, *she never said a word to me, not even in condolence.* It left him strangely sad and wondering why.

Chapter 13

I CONTACTED A SERVICE to arrange a town car for all my ladies of the north end to ride together for the funeral. For the most part, we all felt that attending was the right thing to do, even though there was no love lost among us on Darlene. We were, after all, neighbors.

Once, I had even opened my door to Darlene, although I found her presence in my home brought negative, almost menacing, vibes. At one point, Darlene had expressed interest in my Fun Friday Night Book Club, so I acquiesced and included her in the invite on that occasion.

I remember vividly her attitude from the moment she arrived until I closed the door upon her departure. She arrived that Friday night dressed in a body-slimming DVF wrap dress, gold heeled sandals, and her trademark, bright Italian gold chunky jewelry. Unlike the other ladies, including me, who were dressed in appropriate island, let-your-hair-down garb, she stuck out like a Palmetto Bug in a fruit bowl.

Darlene sized everyone up and down upon her arrival and stated, "Well, this little *par-tay* is a far cry from what I am used to attending on Capri (pronouncing that isle as *caw-pray*)." I remember scoffing at her audacity and told her to sit down and check her ego at the door. As I did so, I caught the eye of Suzy Atwater, who nodded in acknowledgment, and the evening went downhill, fast, from there.

Yet, there we all were, now faced with an occurrence that none of us could have ever imagined. It felt natural to band together in solidarity with each other, but not necessarily in deference to Darlene's departure. After all, she had never tendered respect in life to any of us.

Both the funeral service and the interment were to be held at the gravesite. The temperature for the late-August morning was mild—sticky but tolerable. Most all us gals were dressed in simple black attire; I was sporting my signature "black/white" contrast combo. We were wearing our happy faces, the ones we wore whenever we were together, a trademark feature of the north-end ladies of the island. There was nary a somber face in the car. Bobbi St. John was wearing a black gauze caftan and simple sandals, and looked radiantly photogenic, as usual. I loved being in Bobbi's orbit. Her carefree *joie de vivre* manner always made me feel at ease. Suzy's jittery chatter made for a nice diversion as the town car made its way off-island to the mainland cemetery.

Along with us were the two lawyers from across the street, who were part-timers. Their property shared one small property line with Darlene's. I had heard that Darlene tried to quibble with them at some point over a several-inch encroachment concerning a shared, vacated alley but backed off when she learned the two were both attorneys with deep pockets. I also included another part-timer who was in residence but alone on this visit, Mary Grace Zelmer. While she and her husband, Clark, were generational farmers in the great state of Illinois, they were a big part of the north end of St. Michael's Key. They had invested in developing a group of dilapidated cottages located on the next lane over into three-story homes. Replete with Gulf-view rooftops, their master plan elevated the *Old Florida* homes into a neat enclave that lent itself to hip and cool.

The limo arrived at the interment site and pulled to the curb. Surprisingly, there were quite a few cars lined up and down the rough cemetery road and a group of business-dressed people milling about. Our group exited the car, one by one, as the other attendees looked on. I spotted Detective Cruz off to the side. I started to walk his way when I caught his eye, and he returned a devastating smile. *Geez,* I thought to myself, *that man is handsome.*

"Hey, Cruz," I started as his eyes, somewhat shaded in sunglasses, met mine.

"Hey there, Paris. I see your north-end troupe is all here."

"Yes," I replied. "Our attendance is less for mourning than for our own neighborly accord."

The service began shortly after eleven, so the three canopies provided to cover the fifty-some guests proved sufficient in warding off the rising heat. There were no personal eulogies offered, yet there appeared to be at least a couple of gentlemen family members in attendance, perhaps brothers, brothers-in-law, or cousins. Dressed in black tailored suits and wearing subdued ties, they had *New York* written all over them. Their jackets were fitted to conceal the sidearm pieces I was sure they were carrying.

Behind them, in the third row, sat Nico Stefanos and his mate Gus. I glanced over at Nico and offered him a slight smile; he returned a smile that held a notion of relief to see the face of a friend present at the service.

The priest opened the service promptly and began with a Gospel according to Luke, which seemed oddly off-kilter, given Darlene's mode of living life. From there, he began to talk about Darlene, starting with her childhood and bringing it forth to the present. As the priest crooned on about the perceived successes that Darlene achieved, I knew that the picture being painted was benign in comparison to the truth.

At one point during the service, I looked over at Cruz and caught him staring off into the distance. I knew he was making mental notes of the attendees to use as supporting data for his homicide case. He turned back just in time to catch my glance and, again, delivered one of those amazing smiles. *Whoa,* I thought, *that man can sure pack a "weak in the knees" moment.* Curious, my mind began to wander as I wondered what his backstory was; I made a mental note: *I'll have to look into that in my midnight ramblings sometime,* as I brought my attention back to the burial.

There was no mention of a reception happening at the conclusion of the service, so the gals and I had our driver deliver us downtown to Poet's Corner, a favorite restaurant of mine. Suzy, Bobbi, and Mary Grace ordered a liter of white wine, the attorneys each ordered a glass of red wine, and I stuck with my customary unsweetened iced tea, as daytime drinking had never agreed with me. Loads of Darlene stories were dished that afternoon, and, I must say, the laughter that was evoked from the recounting of these tales was more like *laughing* at Darlene's ridiculous behavior than *celebrating* it.

Chapter 14

As Nico Stefanos made his way back to the sedan he had hired, Detective Cruz approached him. Nico and his friend were dressed in all-black attire and exuded an air of sadness and grief. Cruz introduced himself to Nico and asked if he could interview him, perhaps later in the week. Nico, puzzled by the idea, agreed to meet, and they set the date and time. As Gus and Nico climbed into the waiting car, they displayed parting smiles at Cruz, and it was something about those two smiles that set Cruz's neck hairs tingling. There was definitely something off-kilter in the way they were delivered. *Interesting character*, Cruz thought of Nico, and wondered who the "suit" was standing alongside Nico and what role he might have in this whole sordid business.

Once back at the station, and out of the warm, sticky air and rising temps of the August afternoon, Cruz began to leaf through his notes and fill in his sparse outline. He needed to add some "meat" to this story, and his thoughts ran back to the funeral and specifically to Nico Stefanos. His thoughts were flying . . . so, Nico had cut his European vacation short and returned to pay his respects, even though it was widely rumored that the relationship between him and Darlene was finished. In the mind of a detective, there is always something suspect about the spouse or lover of a murdered victim.

Cruz focused his attention back to the outline he was building and began to pencil in all of the observations he had mentally digested. The pieces were developing, but he was still chasing a somewhat elusive conclusion. Again, his thoughts drifted to the funeral and a scenario he spotted off in the distance that didn't sit right with him. There, at the top of the hill, sat a single black sedan, with one sole figure standing outside, facing in the direction of the canopy over Darlene's coffin. Perhaps the driver was just waiting on his rich customer who had come to place flowers on another grave. He wasn't sure, but his instincts told him to file this observation for future recall.

He moved back toward his desk, deciding to dig into some of his findings. Starting with the gold-lined envelope discarded at Darlene's residence, he pulled up the web page Calendar of Events in the month of August that had been sponsored by the Bird Bay Yacht Club and found one entry that coincided with Darlene's last night on Earth. On the website, there was an entry entitled "The Argyle Foundation Hosts an Evening of Gatsby: Charity Casino Night." The cost for the function was hefty, and Cruz wondered if Darlene was attending as a guest, or perhaps as someone's plus-one, and, if so, whose arm was it she was hanging on to that night?

Chapter 15

Paris

Now that the funeral was over, rhythm on the north end of the island had returned to normal. My routine was facile, so I dug into some assignments that I had been given and began to write. The girls and I still met most evenings up on Little Beach to bid farewell to the day and give thanks for its beauty that was bestowed upon us in its hours.

However, this evening, Suzy Atwater was busy readying for a trip to Texas to visit with her daughter, and Bobbi St. John was working with a committee of ladies in chairing a "40 Over 40: Women of Sarasota" event. So, this particular Sunday evening, I walked up alone. Sunday was always my favorite time to gather at the water's edge. To me, it symbolized a kind of release, where the days of the past week were left behind, their lessons learned and stored away. The days ahead, starting with Monday morning, brought new opportunities to learn, grow, and prosper.

As I walked up to Little Beach the Sunday after the funeral, the beach was unusually quiet. I sat alone in my beach chair, meditating to the natural sounds of the surf and the calls of squawking gulls and herons. An hour into this dreaminess, I smelled a fresh, almost intoxicating fragrance in the air. I opened my eyes and was surprised to see Detective Cruz standing beside my chair, freshly shaven and dressed in khaki shorts.

Startled, I said, "Well, my goodness. I never thought it would be *you* shaking me from my peaceful deep thoughts."

He smiled that mesmerizing smile again and reached down to touch my shoulder. I swear a lightning bolt surged through my loins.

He came back with, "I dropped by your house and figured I might find you here. Would you like to take a ride and grab a drink with me?"

From my dumbfounded state, I awkwardly fumbled with, "You mean like a *date?*"

He quipped, "Well, sure, like a last-minute date with the first person I thought of when I woke up this morning."

Oh, boy, I thought, *his wit was nearly as charming as his movie-star good looks.* With that on my mind, I contained the glee rising in me and gathered up my folding beach chair, all the while displaying my willingness to follow along. One thing was for sure: this was the first time since Harry's passing that

I'd felt an interest of any kind in fraternizing with the opposite sex. Anxious to see where this might lead, I collected my flip-flops from where I'd deposited them at the entrance to the beach and walked one step behind this handsome Pied Piper.

Cruz was every bit the fascinating guy that I was gradually uncovering from my Google searches. He was married once and had a daughter from that union. His ex-wife, I learned, had remarried, and she and her husband were co-parenting along with Cruz in the raising of the child. I'd also read accounts of some of the cases Cruz had handled and how he'd risen in the ranks of the Detective Bureau.

I was somewhat nervous as I climbed into his Jeep, which, I assumed, was his off-duty vehicle. We drove off-island a short distance up to Southside Village, to a laid-back neighborhood brasserie called "Nick's Tavern."

The proprietor, Nick, greeted us at the door and showed us to an open-air table just inside the patio. The bar was filled with singles, and the tables held mostly diners of middle age. It was a comfortable space for two people on a *first date.*

We settled in and ordered two glasses of wine while we perused the menu. Once the vino arrived, the conversation began to flow. I mean, I felt like there was a dam upstream that had just burst—it was one subject right after another. Some provoked laughter; others sparked some deeper thought. Our voices modulated like that of a seasoned radio-duo. It was the craziest feeling I had ever had. Our server stopped by our table, and we ordered Oysters Rockefeller and Truffled French Fries to share; I didn't realize it, but I was getting hungry.

The hours flew by, and, when I looked up and saw the server counting out for her shift and the back stations being refilled, I said to Cruz, "Hey, let's call it a night."

We drove back to my bungalow, still chattering away with an easy feeling. Cruz pulled up out front and hopped out to grab my beach chair from the back. As he turned to hand it to me, he bent down, brushed my cheek with his, and sighed into my ear. No kiss, just that little purr. I was gone, I tell you, past the point of no return.

Chapter 16

THIS NEXT MORNING, Cruz was up at the first flush of daybreak and pumped iron before he headed to the shower. *Last night,* he thought, *was one of the greatest nights I'd spent in a long time. That writer is really cute and so well-read. It was fun to be around her. She has an interesting air of mystery about her. This one,* he brazenly thought, *is not one to throw back.*

Down at the station, a bevy of weekend disturbances had the place humming. While the uniformed officers handled their "collars," Cruz made strides to the detective arena on the second floor. Once at his desk, he began to pound in the data he'd found from the Yacht Club visit he'd made on Sunday afternoon. There, he'd been able to charm a young hostess who had been present the night of the Argyle Gala. She confirmed to him that, yes, Darlene had been there and was with a formally dressed, short-statured gentleman with a goofy demeanor. Cruz continued to pour on the charm and closed the deal by flashing one of his beaming smiles. With that, Cruz walked away with a copy of the security-camera tapes from that night—no warrant required.

Once his notes had been made, he popped the security tape into the machine and let it run. On the screen, at about the 7:40 p.m. date stamp, sure enough, a dazzlingly dressed Darlene floated into the scene. While Cruz watched and scrutinized her movements, he concurred that she sure was a good-looker, although highly embellished by cosmetics and fashion. He watched for another ten minutes; then, in popped a gentleman in a black tuxedo that did not appear to be a custom-fitted ensemble but rather a rental or a cheap, off-the-rack quickie. He was short, as Casey Jean, the bubbly, talkative hostess at the club, had mentioned. His height appeared the same as Darlene, who was wearing 3" heels, so Cruz surmised him to be around 5'7" tall.

As the tape continued, it showed the two figures milling around for more than an hour, talking to various people, and then moving on through the crowd. Sometime during the speeches that began at nine o'clock, Darlene and her escort exited the building, using the side-entrance double doors. With their departure, the tape ended, and so did Cruz's trail. More confounded than ever, Cruz wondered, *Who was that guy Darlene was hanging onto?*

Chapter 17

Paris

Monday's hours flew by as if the clock hands had wings. I had completed several assignments and successfully uploaded them to my editor. My neck was somewhat stiff, and, as I stood to stretch, I could hear a car pull up on the crushed-shell driveway. I peered out the window and caught my breath. It was Cruz, heading up the walkway with a grocery bag, flowers sticking out of the top. I glanced at the clock. It was 4:35 p.m.

As I walked toward the door, I wondered what I would say. I mean, I'd held non-stop inner dialogue in my head with him all day long, and now I was left with nary a thought! I pulled the door open just as he reached the threshold. I asked,

"What are you doing here, Cruz?"

"Why, I'm here for our second date, Paris," he playfully retorted, and that got me laughing.

"Our 'second date'? It hasn't even been twenty-four hours!" I shot back as he placed the bag down on the hall table and gave me a wiggle of his eyebrows.

"Truth be told, I know girls like you have a 'three-date rule,' and I guess I'm just anxious to get past that third-date part!"

I roared with laughter at his originality, and before I thought about it, I stood on my toes and placed a quick kiss on his lips.

"So, whatcha got in the bag, fella?"

We dined that night out on the lanai. With the distant sounds of the shore birds squawking through their feeding hour and crickets proclaiming eventide, it was a good and dreamy backdrop for the day's curtain drop.

I set the table with the white mini-carnations he'd brought and two fragrant candles to keep the light and the mood soft. Cruz grilled two prime New York strips he had picked up at Morton's Beach Market, and I prepared a salad from the greens he'd brought with him. I opened a bottle of Malbec, because I had read that Cruz was of Argentine heritage.

Again, the conversation was plentiful—and playful, too. I felt completely relaxed and at ease even when questions of my past cropped up. It seemed somewhat odd to me, as I had historically and closely guarded the truth of my past with everyone I encountered. With Cruz, however, I found myself revealing more than I normally would allow myself to do.

The evening ended around 11 p.m., and, again, Cruz was a perfect gentleman. There was a lingering hug and a pull-back moment of him looking into my eyes that would have done me in had he not kissed me on my forehead and said,

"See you tomorrow, Paris, because three's a charm!"

And with that, he was out through the door, leaving his intoxicating scent lingering in the hall. *How will I ever sleep tonight?* I wondered.

Chapter 18

Amsterdam, The Netherlands

A DUBIOUS FIGURE LURKED in the corner of Gate 11 in Charles de Gaulle Airport, waiting to catch a KLM flight to Amsterdam. This would be the last leg of his journey. He solemnly watched the flight-schedule board and listened intently as the loudspeaker spewed out arrivals and departures in a myriad of languages.

Even though the mission he had been on weighed heavily on his mind, the desire to arrive in The Netherlands was all it took to clear those demon thoughts. After all, what's done is done, and what's done is what needed to be done. *There is,* he thought, *no going back now.*

Shaken from this preoccupation, he turned his attention to the line forming to board the flight. He moved in the direction of the loading door and slid into the line, keeping his head down low. "Scuse me," he mumbled as he squeezed by other passengers who were in the midst of organizing their bags and documents. Once on board and settled into a first-class seat, a sense of relaxation found him as he fastened his seatbelt and gazed out at the morning sky. *A short flight, and then I will fade into the terrain of the land of the tulips*, he thought. So far, no one was looking for him, and, so far, he was waltzing about scot-free.

Chapter 19

Paris

After Cruz left, I cleaned up the kitchen and tidied up around the bungalow. I was still full of heady feelings and in need of some perspective. I decided to reach out to someone I had never met, yet one who could "talk" me off most any ledge.

Let me explain: Maya Johnson and I are connected in cyber-space, pinioned together by words only. This joining of forces had begun several years ago, after Maya read one of my articles and sent an email to the editor which, in turn, was forwarded to me. Impossible as it sounds, so was the probability of this relationship. To describe her, Maya is the same age as me, an educator, an artist, and an absolute kindred spirit. Our unscheduled email conversations seem to be delivered in angelic time, always when needed the most. She is a confidante of the highest caliber.

I headed back out to the porch, still invitingly warm with candlelight, propping myself up on the chaise lounge with my laptop, and began tapping away. This would be the first introduction to Maya of my new budding interest. Once I shared all I had to spill—the laments, the trepidation, and the gleefulness that I was feeling—I hit "Send," closed my computer, and blew out the candles. Suddenly sleep was overcoming me.

The next morning, I was up early and about to head out the door for my morning ritual when my phone rang. It was Nico Stefanos. I picked it up on the second ring.

"Hello, my friend," I said. "How's it going?"

"Well, you know—it's . . . going. I know I shouldn't care. She never cared about me; it was always about the money with her. But being back on the island . . . I don't know—it seems too still, like it's missing its heartbeat."

Oh, good Lord, I thought, *he is deep down in a rabbit hole.*

I replied, "I am so sorry, Nico. Is there anything I can do?"

"Yes, Paris. How about we catch dinner tonight and commiserate?"

I agreed, although I didn't know how much empathizing I could possibly offer. I held no love for that wretched woman at all.

Chapter 20

Cruz left the station around a quarter to nine the next morning to meet with Darlene's former paramour, Nico Stefanos. He was eager to begin filling in the cracks and spaces in his investigation.

Nico, always debonaire in his appearance, answered the door to his condo and welcomed the detective with his usual degree of charm. The two shook hands and took seats in Nico's elaborately decorated condo, with stunning views overlooking the sparkling waters of the Intercoastal Waterway.

Cruz began with some routine questioning along the lines of "Where were you on such-and-such date and time?" or "What was your relationship with the deceased?" Cruz had learned early in his career that a suspect could be cleared of pulling the trigger, spiking a drink, or stabbing with a knife, but it did not automatically eliminate that person from the accessory or conspirator spectrum.

Once the perfunctory questioning was out in the open, however, the interview took on more of a conversational tone. Both gentlemen seemed to relax at that point. Nico, feeling like he could not be considered an actual murder suspect *per se*, since he was out of the country and nearly 6,000 miles away at the time of Darlene's demise, demonstrated his relief and began an earnest chat with the detective.

"I have thought long and hard on who could have wanted Darlene dead, but I just cannot make sense of any of this, no matter how long I dwell on it. She contacted me last month at my parents' home in Greece, and we talked for more than an hour. She said there was more we had to do together; more we had to share. Try as I might to discourage her from pulling me back in, the hold she had on me was like the grip of the devil."

Cruz interjected, "Did you two make any arrangements to meet?"

"No," Nico responded. "I put her off, saying I would return to the States in a matter of weeks and that maybe we could get together then. That seemed to satisfy her."

Cruz then brought up the infamous lawsuit in which Darlene had sued Nico over the titles to two adjacent properties on the Key, involving millions of dollars.

Nico's face grew despondent, and Cruz could tell he was sick at heart.

"It was a bad time for Darlene and me—that's for sure. She had a lot of influence and support from the County

Commissioners in bringing the suit to trial. In the end, it was a travesty of justice and one that cost me dearly, both financially and emotionally. I mean, most people saw only the outside of Darlene, and that could bring out the fool in most *anyone*.

"But I knew the inner Darlene, the slightly financially insecure widow without any family support, trying to make it with her own kinda-offbeat, delusional façade. That side of Darlene was warm and open to learning and loving, or so I thought."

Cruz probed into Nico's knowledge of any of Darlene's friends, acquaintances, or anyone who might be contacted to get further leads.

Nico did not come up with any but offered, "Like I said, most people only saw that brash outside of Darlene, so she never seemed to forge any lasting attachments. Most business or interpersonal relationships with her would soon become toxic. She was serial in that regard."

Cruz then took another approach: "From my experience, this crime was not random but rather in a more personal manner. Did Darlene mention anyone during the overseas phone call that you two had? Did she mention any plans she might be making or deals she might be working on?"

Nico thought for a moment before answering, "No, she wouldn't have discussed any sensitive points of business she was working on, especially considering my loss in the lawsuit she'd brought against me. She did talk about meeting a new suitor but did not expound upon it, and I believe she was just saying that to get a rise out of me, just like she had done during our time together."

Well, Cruz thought, *this could be a potential area to look at.* He became silent and pensive for a moment as his thoughts went back to asking Suzy Atwater if she'd ever seen anything akin to Darlene being picked up for a date. When Cruz spoke to Suzy initially, he asked specifically about Darlene's comings and goings in the days preceding her death, but he did not probe back several weeks into Darlene's movements.

Every death scene has a timeline, and I need to expand mine if I want to close this case, Cruz imagined. It occurred to him to ask about Nico's friend Gus and how they were related.

"The gentleman you were with at the funeral? Who was that, and was he someone who knew Darlene well?"

Nico replied, "That was my best friend, Gus Papadopulos. We grew up together on Mykonos, but Gus now lives in Athens, managing his father's export business. His relationship with Darlene was only through me."

In tallying up his findings with Nico, Cruz jotted down some final notes and began to make moves indicating the end of the interview. He inquired if Nico would be staying in Florida and found out that he would be. Cruz then handed Nico his card and asked him to stay in contact if he thought of any additional details that might prove helpful.

As Cruz rose to leave the condo, Nico casually mentioned, "I am having dinner with my friend Paris tonight. She lives in one of the bungalows on the same lane where Darlene lived. I will ask her if she knows anything."

Well, that statement astounded Cruz for two reasons: firstly, Paris and he had spent the last two nights together in non-stop conversation, getting to know each other, and Paris had said nothing about a dinner with Nico; secondly, there was that proverbial "third date" he'd had on his mind the entire morning that would now need to be squelched!

Chapter 21

Paris

THERE WERE MANY ERRANDS that needed tending to after my morning beach yoga, and, since I was down near the Village, I thought I'd knock a few of them out before returning to my bungalow.

My first stop was the hardware store to pick up some bolts I needed to fix a wobbly kitchen shelf. As I walked into the shop, Taylor Greene greeted me with a warm hello and friendly wave. Taylor was the son of a beach acquaintance of mine. I'd met Julianne a couple years back, when Taylor was still in high school. I used to see them at the beach and always marveled at their close relationship. I wondered about a father in this scenario, but the presence of a male figure in their dynamic was never mentioned, so I never probed. I walked to the back of the store, where the nails and other fittings were displayed in bins. As I was hunting through the various options, Taylor appeared, offering his help. I explained my project, and he directed me to the correct fitting.

To fill the conversation with something light, I asked Taylor, "Say, I saw you with a cute girl last week out in front of the Oyster Bar. Is she your girlfriend?" Taylor's face blushed, displaying a smile as wide as the Gulf of Mexico itself. "Yes, that's Sarah, and she's special."

I replied that young love was a precious thing to find and that he should invest in it if he felt that she was a keeper! That advice stirred memories in me of Harry and how smitten my younger self was with him. Now, for the first time since Harry's death, Cupid was beginning to awake those stirrings in the undergrowth whenever I found myself in the presence of Cruz.

Taylor brought me back to reality when he asked, "How about you, Miss Paris? You find anyone special?"

I laughed a short, sweet giggle and told him that mature love acted differently from that of a youthful crush, but, yes . . . I did have my eye on someone. Then the conversation turned to the present day and what was lying in store for the both of us.

Taylor explained that, when he got off work at 4 p.m., he and Sarah were heading to the beach to play volleyball and then watch the sunset.

Good plan, I thought. I told him about my dinner plans with Nico Stefanos, which opened up our chat to the topic of Darlene's homicide and possible suspects.

"Yes, I heard her old boyfriend Nico was back in town. I helped his Greek friend, Gus, about a month ago in the store. He was buying all sorts of construction items. This was before Darlene's body washed up out on Sand Dollar Island, so I never thought much about it, but I did ask him if Nico was here and if he would be beginning a new development project. Gus merely said that Nico wouldn't be back until the first week in September. So, I guess Gus was working on something else."

I left the store with all sorts of hypotheticals in my mind and rode my bike up-island, toward home. I must admit I hoped Cruz would call or show up, so that I could breathe in his essence again, but strangely, he did neither. *Ghosting*, I think the young people call it.

I ate my lunch and finished up some outlines for articles due at the end of the month. Then I lay down to take a short power nap before dressing to meet Nico for dinner. In my restful state, I dreamt about Cruz, a fantastical dream of a winding footpath leading to a wishing well and great mountains looming in the distance. Oh, damn my imagination!

Upon waking, I walked to the bathroom in an almost-trance-like state until I splashed some cold water on my face and proceeded to dress for dinner. I chose a simple cotton sundress and sandals and left the bungalow shortly after 5 p.m. Still no word from Cruz. I half expected at least a text, but the phone stayed silent.

Nico, the consummate gentleman, was waiting for me just outside Dean's Waterfront II, so we walked in together and were shown our table overlooking the bay. I kept the conversation on the light side, hoping to momentarily avoid the topic of Darlene and Nico's resultant blues over her demise. That tactic worked seamlessly through most of the meal, but, toward the end, Nico broke down. All I could do was listen as his battered heart poured out its true feelings for her. I mean, try as I might, I just could not understand this handsome, smart, and wealthy gentleman being so besotted with a wanton alley cat like Darlene—especially after she had just swindled him out of a prime real-estate deal. And so, the evening ended on that sour note: Nico, sad to be recounting his feelings over his lost love, and I, sad that my newfound love interest was nowhere to be found.

Chapter 22

CRUZ QUICKLY HEADED BACK to the station after his morning interview with Nico, because, earlier, some presumptions regarding this case were becoming assumptions. Revelations were surfacing that needed to be attached to his timeline while they were still fresh. Several hours slipped by before he realized that he needed to reinvigorate. He thought he would head to McGuire Park and catch a pickup game of hoops to clear his head. There was nothing Cruz liked better than turning off the madness of his job by releasing all those endorphins and leaving them on a basketball court.

As he drove south on the Tamiami Trail, he began ruminating about Paris and wondering if she had any romantic interest in that guy Nico. Though he was not the type to harbor jealousy, the DNA from his Latin roots held tendencies that fueled passion in him. He was feeling the stir of something significant in his rapport with Paris, and he wanted to know if competition should be considered or confronted, as he moved forward in his pursuit.

Cruz was lucky, because, when he arrived at the basketball courts, there were two guys he recognized, looking for a third to join in the next pickup game. He laced up in his sneakers, performed a few stretches, and prepared by warming up at the opposite end of the court. Once the game got into full swing, the sweat and his angst began to pour out of his pores. Nothing like purging useless lamentations from one's thoughts.

After the game ended, Cruz headed back to his house on the mainland to shower and change. When he had learned of Paris's date with Nico, he'd made a call from the station to his ex-wife to ask if he could come by and pick up their daughter, Brookelyn, for a mid-week dinner with Dad.

It was an agreeable plan, and, so, Cruz headed over to their home around 6:30 p.m. Brookelyn came running out of her mother's house, ponytail swinging and her hair bow askew. Cruz was in love with this magical creature he called "Broo Bear."

Brookelyn was now eight years old and cover-girl pretty. She was athletic, like her father, although her sport of choice was soccer. This tiny difference notwithstanding, they were *simpatico* even beyond biology, and Cruz was grateful every day for their relationship. He vowed that, no matter the circumstance, he would always be devoted to Brookelyn and put her needs and sense of security before his own.

Perhaps that's why he had stayed single ever since the divorce: fear of introducing another female to his daughter might cause Brookelyn to harbor feelings that she was being allocated to second place. He just could not have that happen.

Brookelyn bounded into the Jeep with a barrage of questions and topics.

Cruz turned to her. "Broo, you need to take a breath! We have all evening. Now, where do you want to go to eat?"

"Oh, Daddy—I want tacos. Can we go to Señor Miguel's? Then after, could you take me to Target (she pronounced the big-box store name as *Tar-Jay*)? I need to begin building my back-to-school wardrobe, and Ashleigh Harrington just bought the cutest jeans there."

Cruz agreed. "Of course—we'll do it all. Now, buckle up, and let's go!"

Off they went, and Cruz did not give a second thought to Paris being wined and dined by that debonaire *bon vivant* Nico Stefanos.

Chapter 23

CRUZ'S INVESTIGATION WAS IN FULL SWING by the end of the week. Darlene's phone records were in his possession and needed examination. He assigned one of the 3rd-class detectives the task of running some comparisons of repetitive numbers both to and from Darlene's phone.

The report from Dr. Bullock, the pathologist from the Medical Examiner's office, was in as well. Her narrative report began with a cause of death being post-mortem homicidal drowning resultant from blunt force trauma to the back of the skull. The report was long and detailed, but Cruz ran through its salient points with the skill of a seasoned investigator. The condition and intactness of the body suggested the time of death to be around midnight, with the head trauma occurring first, followed by post-mortem submersion.

The toxicology screen was relatively clean, showing only a small amount of alcohol present at her time of death. The report went on to list what he and the ME investigator had determined during the early morning hours at the scene. There was evidence of vast tissue damage to the rear of the skull, with an abraded contusion.

From the crime-scene data, Dr. Bullock expanded her findings during the autopsy to include the discovery of a number of embedded fragments, thus leading to the conclusion that the weapon used was a metal tool or pipe. The presence of ragged defects to the surrounding skin by compression were thought to be attributed to some type of screw threading on the weapon.

The remainder of Dr. Bullock's report was full of scale-ruler measurements, including descriptions of deep scalp hemorrhaging and associated skull fracturing. She had made notations of no multi-organ failure, which indicated that Darlene was dead before she hit the water. Dr. Bullock concluded that the homicidal injuries Darlene's body incurred from lethal blunt force inflicted to the back of the head caused the injury that took her life. In other words, for once in her life, Darlene probably never knew what hit her.

Cruz placed the report and the death certificate in his file and moved to the findings board, on which he entered the newly discovered facts and the approximate time of death. His next big hurdle was to follow the facts already determined and examine the tides and flows of the currents out on the Gulf waters on that ominous day. This would give him some insight as to where the body might have been disposed of before it washed up on Sand Dollar Island.

The next call Cruz made that morning was to the local Sarasota branch of the Coast Guard. He had a contact there in the Law Enforcement Support and Services Department. Cruz made an appointment to visit the office that same afternoon. Walking back to his desk, he picked up his basketball and began dribbling it in place, an action he took whenever he felt the need to shed some nervous energy and to allow his brain to engage in some deep-thought gymnastics, specifically the chasing of all the details of this tricky case.

Once he had mapped out the next steps in his investigation, he turned his thoughts to Paris and wondered if she were thinking of him as he was of her. Dwelling on her date with Nico Stefanos and whether or not that was a developing story, he speculated, *Hmmpf! What's he got that I don't have? Only about a million and one—dollars, that is!*

Chapter 24

Paris

Cruz had not reached out, and I was half beginning to deny that there had ever been a spark of seriousness. I was thinking about calling him with the tidbit of information I learned from Taylor Greene about Gus being spotted buying construction paraphernalia, but I didn't have to stoop that low, for, when Friday rolled around, my phone finally rang.

"Hey," Cruz said as I picked up.

"Hey, yourself," I responded. "How've you been doing? Preparing yourself for that third-date hurdle?"

Cruz laughed, "No, Paris, but I have been thinking about it! Listen, I've been out pursuing details on this case, so I've been wrapped up. I wanted to know if you had any plans for tonight."

As I was wondering what he had in mind, he continued, "The Magic are playing an exhibition summer-league game, and I was wondering if you wanted to ride over to Orlando with me. I'll have you back by midnight."

Wow—I wasn't expecting *that*. I answered, "Sure, that sounds good because I wanted to speak with you anyway. The two-hour drive will give us a chance to talk."

Cruz said, "Great, can I swing by around 4:00 p.m.?"

I agreed.

He signed off the call with "It's a date!"

My brain relaxed as my heart leapt at this last sentence.

The rest of the day flew by. While I was out picking up dry cleaning, I ran into the market and picked up some salami and cheese and some small glass bottles of San Pellegrino. Once back at the bungalow, I changed into my freshly pressed jeans I had just picked up along with a coral-colored peasant shirt. I lightly brushed my hair and casually arranged it on top of my head. A quick swipe of tinted lip gloss, and I was ready. Back in the kitchen, I took out my small picnic pack and filled it with ice packs and my treats. As I zipped it shut, I heard Cruz's Jeep pull up in the driveway. He swung his leg out and I saw he, too, was wearing jeans and had on top a nicely pressed white oxford shirt. There is something very sensual about that combination—business on top, party on the bottom! He looked . . . let's just say he looked good!

We met at the screen door, and he took hold of the cooler bag and my purse as I locked up the bungalow. Once under-way, the conversation flowed as before with the ease of an old friend. When we reached the highway heading north, we began to chat in earnest. The first thing Cruz asked was, "So, I heard you had a dinner date with Nico Stefanos?" His tone took on a little more of a curious, probing tenor than I am sure he intended because he followed it up with, "Nico told me about your plans when I interviewed him." Quick to set the record straight, I shot back, "Not a date, a consolation dinner with a friend. Although I can't say I understand it, he's still smitten with the idea of Darlene and brokenhearted that she is dead."

That explanation seemed to bring even more ease to the conversation as the miles went by. I brought up my conversation with Taylor about Gus's unusual solo appearance in the Village several weeks back, purchasing an odd lot of items. Cruz thought very deeply on this and, as we drove, we began to draw out some scenarios. There was an incredible energy present in the car at that moment, almost primordial in essence, and I was certain I should allow this organic electricity to exist in my world without questioning it.

Once we had chewed on the Gus hardware-store sighting for a while, Cruz filled me in on some details he had learned concerning Darlene's attendance at the Yacht Club function and her contact with Nico while he was in Greece several weeks before the murder. Without giving too much of the investigation away, Cruz relaxed enough to tell me the suspected murder weapon was thought to be some kind of threaded-steel conduit.

Wow, I thought. *I guess someone, whoever it was, told Darlene to pipe down one final time!*

The basketball game was a thriller—I really got into it. I'd always liked sports but much preferred basketball or baseball over football. Cruz's knowledge of the game of basketball was incredible. As we sat in the fourth row, he was calling the plays and the fouls even before the coaches or refs. It was impressive. The game ended with a loss for the Magic, but the excitement was still in the air as we headed out of the arena for the long drive home.

The ride was uneventful. Cruz and I talked about the game for the first hour, and, the second hour, we chatted and listened to music. Cruz stunned me when a Russell Dickerson song began playing—"It's a Good Day to Have a Great Day," and Cruz knew all the words. This guy was speaking my love-language!

Chapter 25

Paris

Cruz called the next morning at sunup. Getting back shortly after midnight had left me not much time for deep sleep. I was awake but barely. He said he was heading over to the Yacht Club at lunchtime to see if he could discover some more details to fill in the timeline of Darlene's movements between the hours of 9 p.m. and midnight on the day of the death.

He said, "I'll buy you lunch."

I agreed with the plan, and we concluded the call. And so it was, as if history were repeating itself, this new interest of mine seemed fated to be. It felt *intended*.

Cruz picked me up in the sedan cruiser, and we headed off-island. We drove through town, crossing over the causeway toward the Yacht Club lot, and we parked in the shade. We took a stroll through the grounds and around the marina before heading into the building. For all intents and purposes, we looked like any other young-professional couple meeting for lunch.

When our meal was over, we headed back out to the marina, as Cruz was following a hunch as to where Darlene might have headed when she left the Club at 9 p.m. that fateful night. Earlier, when we were strolling around, we'd spotted a sign that read "Leisure Club Rental Dock C-2," and Cruz wanted to talk to some of the dockhands while showing Darlene's photo around.

I felt carefree and serene, with the sun streaming down as we walked side by side. Cruz flashed his badge and introduced himself at the dockmaster's office, and we proceeded down the pier toward Dock C-2. Once we reached the gates and entered the code Cruz had been provided, we were in the midst of a lot of activity. It was Saturday mid-afternoon, and folks were stocking their various watercraft with provisions, readying for an afternoon or sunset cruise. I took a side seat to Cruz's queries, letting the statements he was hearing file into my memory for recall later.

Apparently, there were several people who knew of Darlene, but none had seen her on the evening in question. Back at the dockmaster's office, Cruz handed his card to the administrative assistant, whom he asked to let him know if anyone had anything to contribute. As we were leaving, the admin said,

"You might wanna check with Paul. He's the fellow down on the gas dock who has the most interface with the clients. He might know something."

Paul was out to lunch when we checked back, and we decided to wait. Cruz walked over to the refreshment hut and came back with two ice-cream cones.

Boy, oh, boy, I thought. *Could this day get any better?*

Paul came whistling down the dock about thirty-five minutes later, and we were able to sidebar him before he started his shift back up.

Cruz began his questioning with the night of the gala and asked if Paul had been working that evening. The dock-hand told Cruz he was working but that his shift had ended before the affair was over. Cruz then showed him a photo of Darlene. The photo was taken from the videotape Cruz had acquired on his last visit to the Club, so this image of Darlene was the last known photograph taken of her. Paul looked at the photograph and took a long pause but nodded his head in an affirming *Yes.*

Being the silent observer to official police business, I merely listened as Cruz asked his questions.

"So, you did see her earlier in the evening; did you see her arrive?" Cruz wanted to know.

Paul told Cruz Darlene had arrived in a limousine that evening. He said, "I mean that's how I'm certain I saw her; those long legs went on for miles, and the way she came folding out of that limo, I felt like I was watching a Robert Palmer video. The dame was a damn-fine looker, and I'm a man who likes to look."

Cruz gave him leeway, asking for some more leads but fell short when Paul came up with nothing. Cruz flipped his card toward Paul and asked him to call if he thought of anything else.

It wasn't until we began to stroll off that I began thinking, *If Darlene had been picked up by a limousine, where was her car?*

The ride back over the causeway gave me the perfect opportunity to bring up my thoughts.

"What about Darlene's car? Where would it be if she was using a car service?" I asked Cruz, and then I added, "Have you delved into her credit-card transactions to determine if she made a charge for the ride that night? The limo company she used would be able to ID the driver."

Cruz eased up to a red light and turned to me. "For a magazine writer, you sure know a lot about investigation. Paris, you ever do any media reporting?"

I tensed up and began to get that uneasy feeling when someone inquired about my past. I quickly shrugged it off, because, with Cruz, well . . . things just felt different.

I responded with a light tone to my voice, "Yes, I did, early in my career but decided the chase was not for me." An honest, yet deceptive, answer, I guess. Not the best way to begin what I hoped would become a lasting relationship. *All in due time*, I supposed, *all in due time.*

Chapter 26

Paris

CRUZ DROPPED ME OFF AT MY BUNGALOW, saying that he had to head back to the station for a couple of hours. We made plans, however, to reconvene around six o'clock. He talked about having a movie night, but I was harboring the feeling that we would, instead, be getting down to brass tacks.

Alone with my feelings, I began to examine just what was going on between the two of us. Clearly, there was a romantic interest, but was that interest based on loneliness on both sides, or was it deeper than superficial attraction? Or was it just my interest in the investigation that was drawing him to me? As I pondered my thoughts, I kept coming back to a certain feeling of comfort that always seemed to surface whenever we spent time together. I am a tough nut to crack, given the love-tragic start of my youth, followed by my efforts at reinventing myself down on the Suncoast. So far, my strategy at concealing the true reason I stay unencumbered remains unpublished.

At five-thirty, the phone rang, and I reached for it as I was freshening up my makeup and hair. I mean, *come on . . .* more than three dates have gone by, and the opportunity may just present itself. It was Cruz. He was on his way and again, thoughtfully, was bringing dinner, although he did not elaborate. I hung up and headed for the kitchen to chill some wine and set the table. The carnations he'd brought last week still looked fresh, so I added those at the last minute.

About fifteen minutes later, I heard his Jeep pull into the driveway and moved to meet him at the door. Once all his parcels were safely stored, Cruz suggested we walk over to Little Beach and sit for the sunset. Never one to turn that invitation down, I grabbed two chairs from the lanai, and we headed out, taking the 300-step walk over to the shoreline.

We were met by the exquisite aquamarine waters of the Gulf of Mexico merging into the Pass. This had always been my favorite vista here on the Key, watching the waters flow through this channel on their way to the downtown harbor. For a Saturday evening, the beach attendance was as low as the tide.

We set up our chairs in the shade of a Seagrape tree, and I reached into my bag to hand Cruz a sparkling water. We both took a sip and then leaned back and closed our eyes in organic contemplation. The steady flux that was flowing through the Pass as we sat on the shore had ebbed commensurately, so that Sand Dollar Island was clearly revealing itself out in the distance.

When I opened my eyes, I looked over at Cruz and caught him staring off into the direction of the sandbar, his eyes riveted on that unfolding vision. He was reflecting, for sure, and I wasn't certain if I should break that deep-thought meditation. I couldn't discern if he was concentrating on the homicide or on our budding romance, or *both*. It was then he turned to me and uttered,

"I think Darlene may have been out on a boat that night."

I was jolted by that keen observation. I hadn't thought of that angle. Excited by the thought of uncovering more details, a red-hot fervor was beginning to grow within my bones in answer to my desire to be on the cutting edge of the investigation as well as just being there beside Cruz in working through it. It left me wondering if he felt the same way.

As the sun bid farewell to another banner day, we rose, closing our beach chairs, and began the short walk back to the bungalow. It was so strange to me that, in this new quasi-relationship, there was never a loss for words. Our conversation flowed in abundance. Serenity springs forth from affinity, and I, for one, was becoming enmeshed in its tantalizing spell.

Once back at my abode, we began the dance of preparing a meal together. Cruz had brought some sweet Italian sausages and mini-French baguettes. He also opened a jar of fragrant chimichurri, all the while telling me a story of where he'd found the authentic condiment. "My mama's family is from Buenos Aires, and, where she grew up, on the weekends, the extended family and friends would gather in what was called an *asada,* a cookout of sorts. One of the foods I can remember from my visits there as a child were these grilled French-bread sandwiches that held the sausage and chimichurri."

Cruz's story and the wafting aroma of the sausages grilling had my mouth watering. With every passing minute, it seemed, my composure was becoming calmer and more receptive.

While Cruz was assembling the main course, I set about putting together a simple tomato-and-cucumber salad. I lit some candles to further set the mood, and we sat down at my small dining table inside. Our conversation took on a professional, investigative tone without either of us realizing it. We began weighing the known facts vis-a-vis the hypotheticals.

The car? Where could it be? Concerning Gus, Nico's best friend . . . was his out-of-the-blue appearance on the island weeks before the death circumstantial in any way? I mean, at this point, Gus could not be ruled out. Was Cruz's hunch about a boat being involved be something with merit and worth investigating? So many loose ends.

After our perfectly lovely meal, we went out on the lanai with our last glass of wine and continued our bird-dogging. I listened intently to Cruz as he said,

"I keep going back to the tape I acquired from the Yacht Club. Once the speeches began that night around 9 p.m., Darlene and her companion had meandered over to the left side of the hall, near the side exit. That exit leads directly down to the C-2 dock, where the rental boats are moored. The view from the tape shows that the crowd standing on that side of the room was thick, but reason has it that Darlene and her companion slipped out of those doors and went somewhere."

I countered Cruz with another point: "If the two of them slipped out into the night and headed for the dock, wouldn't they have been spotted by someone?"

Quick to respond, he said, "Perhaps, but not necessarily so." Cruz added, "The inky-black shroud of night may have provided them the perfect concealment. I checked, and it was a new moon that night, so there was not a lot of moonlight." With that, he stood, finishing the last sip in his glass, and reached for my hand.

"Paris, this has been my favorite part of the day. Crazy as this sounds, I think I may be falling for you. And since my instincts are on-fire today, I am thinking your interest is running along the same lines. Shall we?"

I rose to meet his embrace, and we kissed—a long, deep, and blissful kiss that was to be the first of many. I reached down and turned off the lanai light as we headed inside. Once down the hall, I closed the bedroom door behind us. Morning would find me a completely changed woman.

Chapter 27

Paris

SUNDAY MORNING STARTED OFF EASILY ENOUGH—nothing had changed, yet everything was different. There were lots of lazy hours, catnaps, and—oh, yeah . . . kisses. There were a few of those! I caught Cruz a couple of times making notes in the little black book he carried everywhere. Other than that, we spent the day in the throes of love as a light rain fell outside.

We decided to have dinner out and headed back to Nick's Tavern in Southside. We chose a corner booth, and we both ordered a burger and iced tea. The similarities that kept cropping up between the two of us were remarkable. As we sat waiting for our order, Cruz brought up the topic of his daughter and shared a photo of her.

"This is Brookelyn. She's eight and the best thing that ever happened to me."

I tenderly held the photo and commented on her beauty. Then I said, "Tell me about her."

Cruz's eyes lit up and softened at the same time. "Oh, what can I say? She's a great kid. She's smart and, like me, loves sports—plus she's got a huge, tender heart. After the divorce, when she was still little, she would say, 'I'm going to marry you one day, Daddy. Then you won't be alone.' I mean, she's sweet. Smart and sweet and wrapped in a pretty package, thanks to my ex-wife; Brookelyn takes after her."

Well, I thought, *if she took after you, that wouldn't be so bad, either!*

The evening sailed right along with a feeling of merriment in the air. The patrons in the bar were lively and added to the vibe. All at once, Cruz reached over and took my hands, saying,

"Tomorrow, Monday morning, back to reality. This weekend has been . . . it's been something special. So, I ask you, Paris, what exactly is this? What do you want it to be? Where do you want to take this?"

I stammered for what seemed like a minute and said, "It's complicated, Cruz, but yes . . . this weekend felt like I was hanging with a tried-and-true friend. The laughs and humor we share only adds to the quietude. Yes, I would like this to be . . . you know, a thing."

"A *thing*?" he questioned me as he broke into a loud guffaw. "Ha! Me and Paris—we decided we are a 'thing'!"

I blushed and brushed aside his attempts to tickle me. "C'mon, Cruz—you know what I meant. Be serious. It's complicated. It's been a 'minute' for me since I've been involved in a relationship. I've been on my own, and there are reasons for that. But this 'thing'—there, I said it again—this *thing* feels very organic to me, almost angelic in sum and substance. I kinda think you were sent to me. Is that possible?"

Cruz pulled me closer in the booth and whispered into my hair,

"No, I think what you are feeling is probably true. I believe in holy spirits, too. So, Miss Paris, let's just do the damn 'thing' and see where we go."

I looked at him and smiled. "Sure, Cruz, but can we start tomorrow? I need to get some real sleep tonight."

Chapter 28

CRUZ WALKED INTO THE STATION early the next morning. *Paris was right*, he thought. *Getting a good night's rest last night was what I needed to function on a full tank today.*

As he walked to his desk, he noticed a stack of files on the corner looking as if they had just been delivered. He immediately headed toward the pile and began to leaf through it. The files contained the data on Darlene he had ordered last week. There were highlighted credit-card statements, bank statements, phone records, and statements from vendors she employed—all interesting stuff. He pulled up his chair and dove in, starting with the credit-card transactions.

The statements went back a few months, so Cruz decided he would walk them forward to see if he could find a pattern. Beginning with the May statement, he found nothing of interest. In June, she had made some unusual charges but nothing glaring. The June statement was satisfied by a minimum-payment-only toward the balance, but the July statement showed a large payment, which not only reconciled the balance but left her with substantial credit going forward. Cruz thought, *Where was the income being generating from?* He made some notations and moved on. He focused on the August statement, scouring each transaction. He was looking for charges for the limousine service, as Paris had suggested, but he found nothing to that effect.

The bank statements were next—and this is where things began to get very interesting. The deposits into Darlene's account were sporadic, with the majority of them made up of cash, not checks. These deposits never exceeded the amount of $10,000, which is a magic number for the Feds in terms of cash transactions. Cruz pulled out a worksheet and began scribbling furiously. Establishing a viable pattern is paramount in any investigation. Human subjects often offer an interesting avenue into their working mind simply by demonstrating repetition.

Once Cruz had compiled his extensive notes, he moved on to Darlene's phone records. This examination uncovered some interesting methods and sequences, specifically patterns that stuck out like a pair of crossed legs sporting unmatched socks. Darlene, beginning with the May statement and moving forward into June, had placed numerous daily phone calls to one particular number, which turned out to belong to a non-traceable burner cell phone.

Then, the pattern repeated itself with the July and August statements but this time to a different burner cell. The duration of the calls was often short, but some of them, especially the ones that occurred deep into the night, were lengthy in duration.

Cruz thought, *Who was she talking to? A confidant? A lover, perhaps?* Then there was the overseas call she'd made to Greece that Nico had confirmed to Cruz. That proved to be a lengthy call as well.

Moving on, Cruz opened the file concerning the local limousine companies in the area. There were four. He made notes in his little black book as to their locations and intended to follow up on all of them. Cruz then went back to the file with Darlene's bank statements and made a list of the cash deposits. He jotted down notes on index cards and pinned them to the Discovery Board up front. An important element to an investigator in trying to get to the bottom line in a case is to "follow the cash"—always follow the money!

Cruz left the station around 2 p.m. and headed up the Tamiami Trail toward the first limousine company on his list. When he arrived, the office was locked, with no one, apparently, minding the business. He opened his book to his notes and called the business number. A voice mail picked up, informing him of special rates for the upcoming Homecoming Season and providing a cell number to call for more information. He then called the mobile number and was greeted by a live person who was not at all helpful. Cruz asked if the office was ever open and received the reply that yes, the office manager would be in tomorrow after 9 a.m.

Cruz left and headed further up the Trail to Bradenton, the next location on his list. There, the office was open, and the phones were manned. *Thank goodness*, he thought. *Not a wild-goose chase this time.* The dispatcher looked over the data that Cruz produced and performed a cross-reference, looking for reservations under the name of "Darlene" or "D'Angelico," which resulted in nothing. Then she plugged in the credit-card number to see if any reservations had been subsequently made. That query hit a dead end, too.

A couple of the drivers were hanging around in the back room, so Cruz meandered back there and started to shoot the breeze with them. He showed them the photo of Darlene and asked if any of them had ever carried her. Most of the drivers had no recall of ever having transported Darlene, but one driver stated that he remembered her, but it was from when he had been driving for another company. Cruz made note of that company, which just happened to be the last one on his list.

After Cruz left company #2, he stopped by the branch of the Bank of America where Darlene had made several of the deposits. Speaking with the branch manager, he questioned him regarding any observations the employees may have had regarding Darlene. The manager stated he knew of her from a transactional perspective only and said he'd observed her to be a neatly dressed and put-together person—although not very friendly.

"She was always in a hurry and sometimes even rude to our tellers, rushing them to do their cash count," he told Cruz.

That sounded about right from the profile Cruz had already established.

Cruz left the Bank and headed back southward toward the Key. The afternoon hours had slipped away, and he wanted to reach out to Paris and see what the evening might promise. As he made his way in the rush-hour traffic, he rang her phone.

"Hey, there. How's your day been going?" he asked when she answered on the first ring.

"Hi, Cruz. It was uneventful, really. I spent far too much time daydreaming about our weekend to have any worthwhile impact on my writing assignments," she lamented.

They chatted some more and planned to take a walk on the beach followed by some Thai food.

Cruz hung up and headed home to shower and change. He was picking Paris up in a little more than an hour and wanted nothing more than to hold her in his arms.

Chapter 29

Investigators and detectives rely on certain instincts. Having a hunch is comparable to what others would call a "premonition." Cruz learned early on in his career that listening to this inner voice would propel him forward more times than not.

After his overnight date with Paris, he left in the wee hours of the morning as she was setting off for the beach to do her morning yoga. The discovery that both of them were inclined to be early risers—those of us who embrace the benefits of being "morning people"—was another commonality about the two of them that he was loving. He swung by his condo to change into business attire, readying his headspace, hopefully to continue the progress he was making in the investigation.

He reached the station about 7 a.m. and started off by ignoring the data files he'd culled through the day before.

Instead, he began establishing a new file that would assimilate his idea of Darlene being aboard a boat on that fateful evening. Of course, as hunches go, there was not much to go on at first, but he parsed on, developing a skeleton sketch of all that he was surmising. Known: Darlene dressed in elegant attire and left her residence seemingly in her car. Known: she arrived unaccompanied in a limousine at the Gala sponsored by the Yacht Club. Known: she was seen entering the Gala through the main double-doors on the arm of a short-statured, unidentified gentlemen.

Together, the two milled about the ballroom for about two hours and then positioned themselves to be aligned by the side-exit doors which led to the rental boat dock. Known: at 9 p.m., when the speeches began, the two vanished, presumably out the side door.

Unknown—well that list was as long as the rap sheet of a career criminal. What Cruz needed to fill in the *Unknowns* was to locate Darlene's vehicle, delve into any boats known to have left the Yacht Club that night, and, most importantly, obtain the identity of the unknown person who Darlene was clinging to that night. *Once I can move these items not yet established into the* Known *category—the writing will be on the wall!* Cruz thought.

Chapter 30

Paris

I took my time with my morning devotion as I felt like I was vibing on some kind of astral plan. I mean, is this what happiness feels like? I thought I knew what happiness was, but this feeling was soul-pumping stuff.

Ever since I left Colorado on that furious day, the day I put the Rockies in my rearview mirror and drove out on a wing and a prayer, I committed to living with gratitude. Grateful that I was able to pack up and "get outta Dodge," so to speak, and thankful that my career allowed me to switch gears and start life all over again. Mindful, too, that my purpose rested in God's providence; that He had a plan for me. This kind of realization makes contentment come without effort.

Refreshed from the mind purge of my morning yoga routine, I sidled up to my computer and started to noodle. Even though Cruz was following his big hunch about Darlene and a boat, he had promised me he would also investigate the odd appearance of Gus on the island a few weeks before the murder. In the meantime, I thought I would check into some of my own notions.

My first thought was to confirm that Gus was indeed here on St. Michael's Key in early August. Harry Burroughs, my deceased ex but whose memory was never buried, had a long-standing contact in the State Department I sometimes leaned on for factoids in my writing. Jhana worked in the Records Review Division and was a great resource for information. Being a writer, I was always grateful for his input. I placed a call to Jhana, and, after at least twenty minutes of catch-up, I gave him the particulars of my call.

I explained that I was following through on an article I was doing about a local murder and needed to know if Gus Papadopulos' passport had been stamped at any time during July and August. Jhana took everything down and said he'd get back to me within several days. This was not alarming, as nothing in the government moves quickly.

Still curious, I began looking into Gus's background. I found he was married, with two daughters, that he lived in Athens and was the Chief Operating Officer for Poulo Oliva, an export company established by his father and of which Gus was the sole heir. There were lots of society postings and photos showing the handsome, tanned Greek, both with and without his wife. The solo photos featured a lot of glamorous smiles of their own.

I was beginning to get the picture—Gus was something akin to a player. There's a certain psychology attributed to wealthy folks. Having money can cloud one's moral judgement, even the well-intentioned and even when a clear line between right and wrong exists. A certain impulse will embolden certain well-heeled folks, and that's when lines begin to blur.

I called Suzy Atwater to see if she'd like to have lunch. We decided to meet at Cafe Serita at 12:30 p.m., so I quickly took a shower, dressed in fresh clothes, and headed out.

Other than a passing friendly wave, I hadn't seen Suzy since she'd returned from Texas. She looked tanned and relaxed.

"How was the visit with the kids?" I asked, knowing I was going to get the story whether or not I inquired. Suzy started off in a torrent.

"Kids, they're great, everybody growing up so fast. You know what they say . . . *great oaks from little acorns grow!* Well, I had a good time, but *lordy*, am I tired and glad to be back to the slow island rhythm. And, how about you Paris, do I detect a glow?" Suzy paused, giving me time to respond.

"No," I said, "I just got a little sun on Saturday walking around the grounds of the Yacht Club."

Well, I'd hardly got those words out before Suzy pounced on me.

"I knew it—my instincts were right! You were on a date, right? Who was it with? Was it the owner of that Jeep parked in your driveway early this morning? Come on, Paris. Give me all the tidbits!"

Well, that is exactly what I *didn't* want to do. I'd spent the last several years on the lowdown; keeping a low profile was now my second skin, so, true to my code, I sidestepped Suzy and her incessant pecking into the inner chamber of my heart and turned my attention to the menu.

"Suzy, your imagination is as deep as one of those caverns you dig in. You are clearly watching too many Hallmark movies! Now, the Grilled Brie and Bacon Panini looks great. Whataya thinking of having?"

After lunch concluded, I set off for the market to pick up a few things that I was out of. I got home around 3:30 p.m. and received a text from Cruz shortly thereafter. The text said he was working a little late and then had plans to pick up his daughter for dinner and would call to catch up after he dropped Brookelyn back at her mother's. I was content with receiving that message—it was delivered in earnest, like we were already beginning to move in the manner of a couple. I turned on some music and began to fix a meal for myself. After dinner, I took a stroll over to the beach to catch the sunset right before it sank down into the granite-gray Gulf waters. I walked back to the bungalow, and, as soon as I opened the door, my phone began to ring. It was Cruz. I settled on a lounge in the lanai, and we talked until midnight. What we talked about for three-and-a-half hours is beyond me!

Chapter 31

For the remainder of the week, Cruz had his shoulder to the wheel. He was pruning the details he had so far and placing them in the timeline he was building. Finally, the gaps were beginning to close. He was still missing some key information, namely the identity of the phantom gentleman with Darlene the night of the Gala. Most probably, this guy had been the last one to see Darlene alive. The attempts at running facial recognition through the Federal LFR system had not turned up any hits. Cruz needed to get back to the remaining area limousine services to see if he could find the driver who carried Darlene that night. Perhaps, when he was able to determine who the driver was, that person would have knowledge of Darlene's other movements, even though she'd arrived at the Gala alone.

Cruz rose from his desk, putting his sport coat back on, and headed out into the Florida heat. He planned to visit the last two limo companies on his list and specifically follow through with the one recommended by a former employee who had previously driven Darlene.

Cruz headed out to the highway and made his way down I-75 to the Venice exit; he meandered around to the industrial park where All-Star Limo Service was located. When he arrived, the office door was open, and there was a valet on the side of the building, washing a white limo. Cruz walked over to the valet first, before heading into the office. He flashed his badge to the flustered lot attendant and began his spiel.

"Hello, I'm Detective Cruz, and I'm investigating a recent homicide. Could I ask you some questions?"

The very nervous peon stammered, "Yes, I guess so."

Cruz continued with the litany of base questions like *How long have you worked here? Do you ever have conversations with the drivers? Do clients ever leave anything behind in the limos that is turned in for possible reclaim?*

The car jockey answered all the questions with more than normal streaks of sweat rolling off his brow. Cruz, doleful that his modest grilling of the fellow was not turning up anything significant, thanked the gentleman as he moved toward the open office door.

Once inside, he met a middle-aged gal with a smoker's voice—raspy and rough, like a growl. She met Cruz's questions with forced politeness.

"I've worked here for fifteen years," she told Cruz, "And I gotta brain that remembers everything. I'm checking through the system I have here, and we have never had a pickup order for a Darlene or D'Angelico, ever. Say, give me her residence and work address, and let me cross-reference that for you."

That search turned out to be a dead end as well. Cruz thanked her for her efforts, and, as he was leaving, she asked him if he could fix a speeding ticket that one of her drivers had incurred.

Cruz turned around and looked at her, saying, "Excuse me, ma'am? Is that really the question you want to ask me?"

The old gal yammered back through a toothy smile, "Can't blame a girl for tryin'!"

Cruz put a call into Paris when he got back into his cruiser. He sat in the air-conditioned car and chatted with her as they made plans for the evening ahead. The relationship they were building was blossoming into something solid. Cruz had put his heart on hold for a couple of years after his divorce. He would neatly arrange things so he had plenty of action in his life to keep him busy and content. But with Paris, he was now ensconced in a relationship that had materialized out of nowhere and seemed to be building its own *impetus*. "It feels right as rain," he told himself over and over again.

Cruz's last stop for the day was to Elite Town Car Service, which was located further north on the Tamiami Trail. As he made his way up the road, he organized his thoughts. Elite Town Car Service was the name of the business where the driver he spoke to remembered carrying Darlene at one time. It was also the last company on the list, so he hoped he'd have better results. He was due for a streak of good luck.

From all appearances, Elite was a nicely presented business. The lot where the building was located was neatly manicured, and the business signage was stylish and classy. Cruz parked the cruiser in the shade and walked toward the building, taking notice of the lot and the fleet of empty vehicles. Once inside, he found a gentleman behind the desk, entering invoices from the stack beside his computer. As Cruz approached the desk, the guy turned and raised an eyebrow at the shield Cruz flashed in his face and gave his full attention.

"My name is Detective Cruz. Say, I am working on a homicide investigation, and I'd like to ask you some questions."

The employee replied, "Hey, Detective. The name is Joseph Russo—'Joe,' really. Sure, pull up a seat."

"This is a nice place of business," Cruz began. "How long have you worked here?"

"About nine years," Joseph responded. "The owners are nice guys. They gave me a job when I was down and out—sorta took me in and taught me the business. I started off in dispatch, and now I run the front office."

Cruz cut through the chatter and went right to the chase. "I am trying to find out information on a Darlene D'Angelico and if she was ever a client of this company."

Joseph's answer was golden.

"Sure, she is—or *was*, I guess I should say. We all read the news of her death; she drowned, right?"

Cruz answered without commentary. "I'm actually working on an investigation into her death. I'm curious if your records might show that she hired a car to drive her on the night of August 10th."

Joseph didn't turn toward the computer, as Cruz expected he might, but instead offered, "'Lady D'—that's how we refer to her around here. She is Fredo's client. Fredo is one of our owners. He has been driving her for years. They have a special arrangement."

"A 'special arrangement'? What does that mean, exactly?" Cruz probed.

"Well," Joseph started, "all I know is that 'Lady D' is never put on the manifest. Whenever she needs car service, she calls Fredo directly. Fredo lets the dispatcher know which car he will be taking, and then he drives the dame himself."

"Is Fredo here?" Cruz inquired.

"No, sir. He's on vacation, but his brother Franky is around—I can have him call you," Joseph replied.

Cruz was nowhere near done with his questioning, so he continued.

"Can we check with dispatch and see if they show that a limousine was assigned to Fredo on the evening of August 10th?"

"Sure, let me call over to the driver-dispatch shack."

As Joseph reached for the desk phone, Cruz interrupted his thought. "Don't bother. If you point me in the right direction, I'd like to speak with dispatch directly."

Cruz headed across the tarmac to a small building located in the rear lot, which was filled with about ten Lincoln Town

Car sedans, four full-sized black Cadillac limos, and one candy-pink stretch limo. *Wow, a 15+ vehicle fleet with a cherry on top,* Cruz thought comically, *and . . . where'd that Pepto Bismol-colored jukebox come from—the Mustang Ranch in Vegas?*

When he entered the shack, there were three drivers sitting around watching a golf match on television. Behind the dispatch desk sat a heavy-set man with crooked teeth. Cruz approached and introduced himself. The man identified himself as Paul Gallo, and Cruz flashed his badge once again, announcing his name as well.

"I need some information on a client pickup from the night of August 10th." Once Cruz spelled out the details of what he was looking for, he received the same answer as that from the front-desk clerk, Joseph.

"That's Fredo's ride," Paul told Cruz. "You'd have to speak with him about that."

Cruz pressed on, undeterred by this deflection. "I understand that Fredo, your owner, is not available at this time; so, buddy, let's just work with what we have. You have the info on the vehicle that Fredo assigned to this client pickup, right? Can you show me which vehicle was involved? Also, would anyone else here at Elite be in a position to know where the pickup was scheduled to take place?"

Gallo replied, "Like I said, Detective, I'd like to help you, but you really gotta talk to Fredo. It's his business, and he always handled all the rides for that lady himself. I do know that he took the black stretch that night, because I had it scheduled for a group of teens going to a sporting event, but

Fredo had me put them in a smaller limo, so that he could use the stretch. Fredo said to me, 'Lady D needs a showy ride tonight,' so I didn't question it further."

Cruz nodded, all the while making copious notes in his black book. When Cruz had exhausted every query he could muster, he turned to leave, thanking Paul for his input.

Back in the front office, Cruz found Joseph still going at the stack of invoices.

"Joseph," he started, "how can I get ahold of Franky? When will he be in the office?"

"Tomorrow morning, first light of day," Joseph replied. Then he added, "Franky is the early bird, and Fredo is the night owl. I guess brothers come in all shapes and sizes. As partners go, though, they are a perfect fit."

And with that, Cruz left the shop and continued back north toward the island, calling an end to the day, the wheels of progress in his investigation finally turning his way.

Chapter 32

THE EVENING STARTED OUT about as picture-perfect as even I could imagine. Cruz arrived just after the sun dropped down, the sky still redolent with smoke and plum wisps. I ordered pizza from Claudio's, which I now had warming in the oven, and made a garden salad that I had chilling in the refrigerator.

I was really beginning to relax in this new romantic kinship that was developing between Cruz and me. I mean, since Harry, I had held a "no interest" attitude when it came to opposite-sex advances, preferring instead to remain merely empathetic, with my head down, a solo profile fitting me just fine. Now, along comes this electrically charged, handsome man who appeared out of nowhere, investigating my dead neighbor's murder, and I fall for him. And, like my deceased boyfriend, Cruz is a cop. I'm not sure how this attraction even happened.

When Cruz waltzed in the door after giving a short rap, I spun around and planted a kiss on him. He returned the favor, and we began to sway (I told you it was a perfect night).

After the passionate niceties were over and we were both wearing smiles, I put out our food and served wine and sparkling water. As we ate, we chattered on and on about every topic imaginable and spent a lot of our exchange on the ever-present topic of "Who killed Darlene?" One thing could be said about this relationship: we never seemed to run out of dialogue.

Before long, we both grew tired. I cleaned up, and we turned out the lights on the day. As I turned down the bed, I thought, *We both accomplished a lot today. Cruz made strides in his investigation, and I made to a step toward letting go of the past.* Now, *that's* momentum.

Chapter 33

Morning had barely dawned when Cruz woke first, rousting the sleepy-eyed Paris out of her slumber.

"I gotta run, Paris," Cruz said. "I've got an early bird to run down."

He kissed her hair-tousled bedhead and headed out the door. As he drove the cruiser down the lane, his detective-radar was not yet awake, and he never noticed the prying eyes of Suzy Atwater.

Even at that hour of the morning, Cruz got off the island and over to his condo in record time. He strode into the building and made his way to his unit in time to hit the gym before any other tenant could beat him to it. Toward the end of his routine, a tall fellow sporting a bald head came in and gave him a nod. Cruz smiled back and finished up. He was in a hurry and was focused on meeting Franky, the owner of

Elite Town Car Service. *I've got to close some gaps*, he thought as he slung his pack over his shoulder and headed upstairs to hit the shower.

Cruz arrived at the Elite property just after 7:30 a.m. Joseph arrived in the lot just as Cruz was pulling the cruiser in. Joseph greeted Cruz and walked ahead toward the office. Cruz sauntered in moments later, after a brief viewing of the outside surroundings.

"Say, Joseph, I thought I'd drop by early and catch Franky. Is he available?"

Joseph answered that he thought Franky was in the kitchen and that he would check. Joseph walked down the hall, and, after a moment, he called to Cruz to join him. Cruz found both gentlemen in the kitchen, making coffee; he introduced himself to Franky, who smiled and offered him a cup. Grateful for the caffeine injection, Cruz settled into a seat across from Franky, and Joseph returned to his front-desk domain.

Franky had all the outward appearances of a decent guy. His answers to Cruz's questions were forthright and came easily, and it appeared to Cruz that Franky and his limo business were both on the up-and-up. Franky answered everything he could about Darlene, though his knowledge was limited. Yes, his brother Fredo had an arrangement with Darlene. Yes, they dealt directly with each other, never through the staff. Yes, records show the black stretch had been taken by Fredo that night and returned later, around 2:30 a.m. The stretch was then cleaned and went out on another rental the following weekend. Cruz, advancing the questioning to the present, asked,

"Could I see the stretch, Franky? I mean I know it was assigned out and cleaned on return, but I'd still like to have a look."

Franky rose and walked to the back wall of the kitchen. He opened a large metal box that contained hooks that held the keys to the fleet. Once he identified the correct fob, he motioned to Cruz to follow him.

The morning sun was beginning to beat down, even though the hour was close to 8 a.m. The two men walked on the treed side of the lot to take advantage of the shade, and, as they rounded the corner, Cruz spotted the only black stretch in the lot. Franky hit the fob, and all the doors unlocked for them.

Cruz started his examination with the first seat he felt that a lady might take riding solo in a limousine, the woman he imagined from Pete's description from the gas dock at the Yacht. He took out his pen light and carefully ran it over the surface of the carpet, brushing his hand lightly over the nap to see if anything surfaced. Then he directed his light to the seat crevice on the driver side, carefully pulling back the leather to see further down.

Next, his light beam went to the headliner material, where he spotted a long blond hair caught in between the liner and the window binding. Carefully, he removed the hair with tweezers and placed it into a bag that he then dated. Cruz moved on, looking over every nook and cranny of the limo and even examining the trunk. He didn't come up with any-thing else, so the two men headed back across the lot to the air-conditioned office. As he pulled up a seat, Cruz began with,

"Can you pull up how many times the stretch has been booked out since August 10th?"

Franky moved over to the computer and produced a log. "Looks like it was sent out on three calls since Fredo took it out in August—one was to a golf foursome who needed a sober driver, and no one in the group wanted to be the designated, so they hired a limo. The second hire was to a couple of baseball executives here from Camden Yards in Baltimore who were heading over to Ed Smith Stadium, the Orioles' Spring training headquarters, and the last one was an airport pickup of some celebrity's kid home from military school."

Cruz thought about it and became certain that the hair he'd found belonged to Darlene, as no other female passengers had ridden in the stretch since Darlene's death. Cruz then got to the subject of Fredo—specifically, where he was vacationing and when he was coming back.

Franky was earnest in his answer, yet Cruz detected a change in his demeanor.

"He went to California and Vegas," Franky told Cruz. "Fredo loves the nightlife. Oh, well, *to each his own,* right? He's my brother, but we are two different people—*like day and night*, my mother used to say, God rest her soul."

Cruz asked again when Fredo would be back, to which Franky replied,

"It was supposed to be next Monday, but he called me and let me know he was extending his time . . . met a live one, I guess. I now expect him back here by the end of the month."

Cruz collected Fredo's cell number from Franky and thanked him for his cooperation. Once back in the cruiser, heading for the station, Cruz placed a call to Fredo. It went right to voice mail. As he looked at his watch,

Cruz said softly to himself, "The sun is already up on the west coast. I guess Fredo and his *live-wire* haven't raised the shades yet."

Chapter 34

THE REMAINDER OF THE DAY found Cruz spending time at his desk, undertaking the task of identifying the man on Darlene's arm on the night of her death. The only image he had of him was upon his entering the Gala and sidling up to Darlene. The techs in Cruz's department had zoomed and cropped the footage as best they could, but there was not enough clarity, apparently, to get a facial-recognition hit.

Cruz remembered that there was a camera centered at the front entrance of the Yacht Club, accounting for vehicles coming and going. For that footage, Cruz would need a subpoena. He signed into the computer and saw that the film was logged as "now available." Cruz decided to take a ride to the Yacht Club and retrieve it himself.

As he drove his Jeep around the tidal basin of the bay, he headed toward the causeway. He took the time to admire the sheer beauty of the blanket of shimmering diamonds sparkling on the water. His thoughts then moved to Paris and Brookelyn and his desire to have them meet. He knew instinctively that they would get along. There was just a sense of peace about Paris, and knowing Brookelyn's quest to see her dad happy, well . . . Cruz knew his smile was genuine whenever he was in Paris's presence.

Cruz pulled up to the Yacht Club and parked. He headed into the front entrance and up the stairs, just in time to spot Casey Jean readying to leave. Cruz approached her station and caught her eye. Casey greeted him with,

"Hello, Detective. How can I help you today?"

Cruz answered, "Thanks. I see you're getting ready to leave for the day. I'm here to pick up an envelope that is said to be ready."

Casey turned from her station and motioned to a burly gent in the hallway.

"Hey, Brett. Can you help this detective?" She then turned back to Cruz and said, "Sorry, Detective. I've got to run. I'm registering for school this semester and have to make it to campus for initiation."

Cruz returned her parting smile and turned his attention to the brawny fellow in front of him, who inquired,

"Can I help you, sir?"

Cruz noted the name badge identifying Brett as *Security*. Cruz displayed his own shield to the gentleman out of respect and explained to him what he needed.

Brett nodded as he excused himself and headed down the hall toward the General Manager's office. He was gone only a minute and came out with a bulky Manila envelope in his hand.

"Let me know if you have any questions or need more information, Detective . . . happy to help. Our guests' privacy is of utmost importance to us, but I do understand you're on a case."

Cruz thanked him and moved back toward the front doors. Once back in his car, he felt a burning desire to get back into the case. He spun the Jeep out back over the causeway and headed to the station as the afternoon sun was beginning to sink down. On the ride, he reached for his phone and called Paris. She didn't pick up, so he left her a message not to expect him in person but that he *would* call later.

Back at his desk, with the tape machine operating, he began the laborious process of weeding through hours of footage. The camera's position had captured all vehicles entering and exiting the Yacht Club on the evening of August 10th. One by one, he stopped and zoomed in on every car, scrutinizing every driver and passenger.

Cruz was at it for more than two hours before he rose to stretch and get a cup of coffee. He looked outside at the pitch-black and glanced at his watch. *Jeez*, he thought, *I'd better call Paris.* He dialed the number, and Paris picked up on first ring.

"Hey, Cruz," she purred. "I missed you today. Sorry I missed your call, too. I was out in the yard, shooting the breeze with Bobbi St. John, my neighbor, and I left my phone in the bungalow."

"No worries, baby," Cruz uttered back softly. "I'm still at the station, going through mountains of new videotape that came in from the Yacht Club. I just wanted you to know I was missing you, too."

The two carried the conversation along and then hung up with a plan to meet the next day for dinner. Cruz told Paris he had something he wanted to talk about and suggested they cook at home. It was a good plan and one that both looked forward to.

Chapter 35

It was 1 a.m. when Cruz finally reached his condo. Dog-tired, he dragged himself in and headed to bed. His eyes were strained from scrutinizing the many hours of footage. He was successful in making it through to the end of the tape but was not able to pull out any gent matching Darlene's escort that fateful night. It was late afternoon when he finished with the first run of examination, but he decided to cue it up and start again, this time beginning with the entrance of Darlene's limo and moving forward from that point. His thought was that Darlene had been present at the Gala for at least fifteen minutes before the gentleman appeared at her side. Therefore, it made sense to Cruz that the gentleman's car would have come through the entrance after Darlene's limo had made its way through.

Cruz fell into a deep sleep and, for hours, dreamt about some fictional gruesome disturbance. When the sun came up, he woke with a start, his body in a full sweat and his heart pounding. Nightmares were something he'd never been plagued with, yet here he was, trying to shake the appalling, ghoulish nightmare from his memory.

A quick shower restored his lucidity, and, rather than head out to the station immediately, Cruz made a cup of coffee and took it outside onto to his balcony. He returned his thoughts to the investigation, and, as he sipped the dark brew, he wondered if his strategy needed to be redirected. With his last reflection satisfying him that the track he was on would be fruitful, he returned the coffee cup to the sink and picked up his keys. It was going to be another long day, but, at the end, there would be a lovely woman waiting for him with open arms. Now, that was a pleasing thought to keep him motivated all day.

Cruz arrived at the station around 8 a.m. with a burning idea on his mind. Once at his desk, he began to view the same tape he had pored over the night before, but this time, he paid careful attention to Darlene's arrival as her limo pulled into the Club. He fast-forwarded, stopped, rewound and stopped, and then zoomed in on Darlene's driver. *Hmmm . . . Fredo matches the build of the man on Darlene's arm, and it appears as if he is wearing a rumpled tuxedo shirt.* With a couple more taps on the device, particularly a zoom into the frame, he was able to see a tuxedo jacket hanging on the valet hook.

"Son of a gun," Cruz cursed. "Darlene was attending the Gala as if Fredo were her escort, instead of her chauffeur. My, oh, my—that's some cunning dame." Now, the big questions bouncing around in Cruz's mind were *Where did the two of them go when they disappeared from the Gala? What were they up to?* And, more importantly, *Was Fredo the one who killed Darlene?*

Cruz grabbed his basketball and began his idle dribbling. After about a half hour of driving his co-workers out of their minds, he decided to head out to the courts at Arlington Park for a shootaround. It was a short drive from the station to the courts, and, by a stroke of luck, he was able to park right in front. One of the two single-backboard practice courts was available, so he headed that way and got his game on.

Sports had always been something that made him come alive. He found a certain freedom in it, especially given his chosen career. He dealt with many unpleasant aspects of life, and he always felt that, if he let the rigors of the job get to him, it might pull him down, too. So, letting off steam not only strengthened his resolve, but it also brought him to an even keel.

As Cruz shot his baskets, one right after the other, dancing around the back court, his mind wandered to Brookelyn. His daughter shared his passion for all sports, and that brought him a feeling of pride. Starting to get winded, he slowed his pace and made a few more shots before calling it quits. He headed over to the shade and sat on a bench to cool down. Paris had been expecting his call and had agreed that they could share a meal at his place for a change. His thoughts went to food first and then to Brookelyn, as he wondered if tonight would be a good time for her to meet his love interest. He thought it might.

Cruising back to his condo, he stopped at Whole Foods and picked up some shrimp and some fresh produce. His daughter loved Gulf seafood. Once in the condo, with all the groceries put away, he reached for his phone. First things first: he called Paris.

"Hey, baby," he began.

"Hey yourself, Cruz. It's still early. I didn't expect to hear from you until a little later. What's up?"

Paris had a singsong way of speaking that carried a melodic cadence. Cruz couldn't contain his grin as he listened to her.

"Remember I told you that I wanted to talk to you about something?"

Paris hesitated. "Yes."

"Well, can we talk about it now?"

Again, Paris paused. "Yes."

Then Cruz hit her with, "How would you like to meet my daughter, Brookelyn? If you say 'Yes,' how about you meet her tonight?"

Chapter 36

Paris

THE PROSPECT OF MEETING CRUZ'S KID was both daunting and exhilarating. I had always enjoyed meeting and conversing with new people and found young people most interesting for their revolutionary viewpoints on life. But an eight-year-old? Would we find common ground? Would Cruz's easy demeanor suddenly change because his "cub" was in the mix?

Having chosen to be somewhat segregated in my self-imposed exile, any thoughts of children or a family were buried deep within me. It's not that I took a stand or *chose* childlessness. It was that I chose to live a secluded life by way of circumstance, and that was what had led to my present hermitic lifestyle.

However, Cruz was different; this feeling about him and thoughts of where it would lead were different from anything I had encountered since Harry's passing. It felt organic—orderly, like a nice, tidy sequence. I vibe to a natural structure, even though, on the outside, I appear as if I am spirited and free.

Cruz brought that comfort to this budding relationship right from the first day he'd made his interest known. He'd built a rhythm into his communication style; calling or texting at a regular pace, he demonstrated his attention with his conversation and his thoughtful actions, neither of which were contrived; they were offered as a genuine, inbred quality. "Cruz really does speak my love language," I murmured out loud to no one nearby. "This is soul-mate stuff!"

The rest of the afternoon flew by as I readied for this important meet-and-greet. I chose wide-legged faded jeans and a navy V-neck Tee, which I paired with simple, layered gold chains around my neck and beaded bracelets at my wrist. Then I added some gold flat sandals. Checking my reflection in the mirror, I thought I looked young and cool. "I hope Brookelyn thinks so, too," I murmured to myself.

I reached Cruz's condo about 6:30, arriving on time, as was my custom. I took the elevator up to the 9th floor and nervously double-checked my appearance in the elevator's reflective door. With a deep breath, I lightly knocked on the door and heard an immediate stampede of footsteps heading toward me. The door opened to the most adorable child, with brown curly hair streaked with golden threads. She bore a smattering of freckles that were beginning to fade from her maturing face but were still present enough to give her that childish glow.

"Hi, Miss Paris," Brookelyn trumpeted and threw her arms out wide for a hug.

"Well, hello, Miss Brookelyn. *El gusto es mio.*"

This captivating youngster replied in perfect Spanish, without skipping a beat, *"Pasa, por favor—es bonita, papá,"* winking at her father.

I tell you, I was under her impish spell before I could even put my purse down!

It had been a while since I'd had any interaction with a child, but the energy in the room was thick with exuberance, and I fully relaxed into it. We started off with the three of us in the kitchen. Brookelyn asked for my help with arranging some appetizers. The two of us chatted as I explained to her that meat-and-cheese platters were often referred to as *charcuterie,* a term derived from two French words meaning "cooked meat."

I found it refreshing that Brookelyn held onto every word I spoke with fascination, and we conversed without the slightest hint of a generational gap. Cruz kept glancing over from his prep area, smiling, nodding, and contributing when he could get a word in edgewise. The energy in the room was the same as the vibration I had been building with Cruz when it was just the two of us, yet this energy was enhanced.

Could this be what having a family would feel like? I mused, not knowing what to make of that idea.

After about an hour of the three of us chatting and nibbling, Cruz called for us to take our seats, so we moved to the dining-room table that Brookelyn had set. Cruz brought in a huge pan filled with pasta and shrimp in a white-wine cream sauce, with peas, mushrooms, and asparagus. He served us each a bowl, brought a plate of garlic bread to the table, and sat down. When I tell you the idea of a handsome man who can cook "gourmet" thrills me, well . . . it's a concept most gals are afraid to even dream about!

While I was still thinking that thought, Brookelyn turned to me with raised eyebrows and said, "He cooks like a chef—whataya think about that?"

I'll tell you what I think, kid—I think you and me think a lot alike!

Chapter 37

THE EVENING COULD NOT HAVE GONE BETTER. Cruz and Paris cleaned up while Brookelyn did her remaining homework, and, after a pleasant chat out on his balcony, Cruz and Paris both rose to leave. Cruz had to drive Brookelyn to her mother's home, as it was a school night, and Paris was heading back home. The evening had been brimming with enough stimulation to last through the night.

The next morning, the alarm went off with a shrill just as the sun broke over the horizon. Cruz had rested peacefully—no pesky dreams to break his deep delta sleep. He rose quickly and reached for the weights in the corner of his room. Once pumped enough to get his juices flowing, he hit the shower, anxious to reach the station early. He needed to set up a meeting with Franky to get the *skinny* on his brother. Surely, if Fredo was involved with Darlene in ways other than as her driver, it's possible her demise could have stemmed from a domestic argument or lovers' quarrel. Cruz needed to delve into Fredo's character, and what better way to open up that worm can than to have a "question and answer" session with his big brother.

After Cruz reached the station, his first call was to Elite Limo, where Joe Russo answered the phone.

"Hello, Detective," Joseph said. "Sure, Franky's here. Let me get him for you." Cruz held on while Franky was summoned. Within a minute, Franky cheerfully answered the phone. Cruz asked if the two of them could meet and arranged to have coffee at a nearby sandwich shop at 11 a.m. Next, Cruz called Paris because he just could not contain himself any longer—he had to know what she thought about the evening with his daughter!

Once Cruz had finished his telephone call with Paris, he picked up his sport jacket and headed for the door to meet up with Franky. His thought was that Franky would be more open to converse freely without the listening ears of his employees.

He reached the sandwich shop just before 11 a.m. Given that the hour was still before noon, the lunchtime rush had not yet arrived. Cruz walked to a back booth in the restaurant and ordered two coffees just as Franky appeared.

After shaking hands, Cruz jumped right into interview mode. He explained to Franky that, from all appearances, it was believed that Fredo not only drove Darlene the night of the Gala but had also escorted her into the affair. Franky seemed gobsmacked at that revelation. Cruz probed deeper into Fredo's personality and perceived that, between the two brothers, Franky was the sensible one, and Fredo was what one would call the "wild child," not exactly the type you want coaching pee-wee soccer.

Franky explained that, in all their years of growing up together, his younger brother Fredo was always one to "push the envelope"; in other words, his maxim in life was "I want more," whereas Franky was always content with what he had in the present.

Franky, almost sad in his recount of their formative years, stated that his mother was often exasperated in trying to keep Fredo from getting into trouble. The boys were very young when they lost their father, and their mother had her hands full raising the two single-handedly. As they conversed, Franky displayed no signs of lying; his patter was in normal rhythm, and he was relaxed as he reminisced about growing up with his brother in Hoboken, New Jersey.

"Mafia was still around; it was ever-present," he said, despite the cleanup by the Waterfront Commission in the late 1970s. "It was a time in life," Franky explained, "that loads of *goods* were either being run from docks or being hijacked from trucks in lower Brooklyn, Staten Island, and from the north Jersey shore. "It was quiet, but it was still going on.

"That was . . . ," Franky explained, "why my mother packed us up and headed to Florida—to reestablish ourselves away from the flirtations Fredo was making with the gangster life." Franky went on to say that, after a few years in the Sunshine

State, he met and married his wife, subsequently producing a nice little family.

But Fredo, on the other hand, stayed restless, never wanting to settle down. "If truth be told," Franky declared, "Mother's subsequent death was probably due more to her broken heart than to emphysema."

Cruz made his notes as Franky chatted on, explaining that the limo company had been born out of the funds of his mother's estate, and the rest, he said, was history. Fredo and he were great partners; the value of what each man brought to the table made for good synergy—the *Yin* and *Yang,* he concluded.

Cruz redirected his questioning, asking specifically if the two brothers had ever discussed any personal involvement concerning Fredo and the deceased.

"Do you know if Fredo was enmeshed with Darlene in any other manner besides strictly business?" Cruz inquired.

Franky merely shook his head from side to side, indicating a *No, I don't know.* Cruz then probed as to the frequency of Darlene's requests for Fredo's services; Franky told Cruz that it was a couple of times a month.

The conversation then turned to Fredo's anticipated return; it was nearing the end of September, and Fredo would soon be coming back to work.

Franky said, "Yes, Fredo is scheduled on a flight from Las Vegas arriving on Southwest Airlines at 10:20 p.m. the night of September 30th," a mere nine days away. Franky said, in an earnest, truthful manner, "Fredo's been gone from the helm for a while now; it will be good to have him back. Things just seem to work better when we're both on the job."

Cruz closed his black book and indicated to Franky that his commentary had been a big help in trying to understand why Fredo was at Darlene's side attending the Gala instead of in the limo lot, awaiting her departure. Cruz told Franky he'd be back in touch and would follow up with Fredo upon his scheduled return, as all attempts at reaching Fredo through his cell number had been going unanswered. Franky's eyebrows raised at that declaration.

Strange, Cruz thought, feeling uncomfortable. *This whole entanglement with Darlene and Fredo is abnormal. When clues leave you feeling like a stranger in a strange land, that's when a case really gets mystifying.* Prosecutorial cases involving homicide—but lacking eyewitnesses—are like telling a "story," a story that has its fair share of gaps and holes.

Chapter 38

Paris

THE PHONE RANG LATE IN THE AFTERNOON while I was cleaning up my studio. The call was from Jhana, at the State Department, with the information I had requested on Gus Papadopulos. After Jhana and I had chatted, he gave me the travel stamps recorded on Gus's passport. Jhana read the data to me.

"Mr. Papadopulos entered the United States through the port of New York on July 14th, stating that his entry was for the purpose of attending to business at the Jacob Javits Center. He listed his business as the company, Poulo Oliva, which allowed him to travel into the States under an electronic eSTA visa, permitting him up to 90 days to conclude his business.

The next stamp was a re-entry stamp upon his return to Greece on July 25th. His re-entry documents were all in order and, thus, his return uneventful.

Jhana then gave me some information, which, although peripheral, was still somewhat illuminating. He said that Gus's departure from the States was not from the port of New York, where he had entered, but from the port of Miami. My eyes opened wider as I coupled this information with Taylor's sighting of Gus on St. Michael's Key during this same time frame.

So, I thought, *this confirms that Gus was in Florida at some time in July.* The questions on my mind were, *Why was Nico Stefanos' best friend from Greece on St. Michael's Key without Nico?* and *What was the purpose of his unusual appearance here?*

I finished up all my tasks and was beginning to get anxious that I had not heard from Cruz. About a half-hour later, he texted that he was on his way over and that I should decide on what I would like to do that evening. I had been thinking of Vietnamese Pho all day, and, so, we decided we would take a short drive down to Castle Key, where I knew a great spot to park and watch the sunset over the Gulf.

From there, we could drive back toward Sarasota to a friend's southeast Asian bistro that served Pho and share a meal and a pot of jasmine tea.

When Cruz arrived, he was all in favor of my plan. *Again*, I thought, *how refreshing it is to commune with someone like him.* Shortly after his arrival, we headed back out, waving to Bobbi St. John as we passed her car coming down the lane. We reached Castle Key in about twenty minutes, which was in perfect accord with the setting sun. We sat in his Jeep with the sides zipped out and let the Gulf breezes and the magic of the sunset grace our comportment. This was one custom Floridians adhere to—taking time to give thanks for the day. Most often, locals will find their way to the water's edge to pay homage while the sun makes its final curtain call.

Sitting and relaxing with Cruz in the Jeep, with my feet up on the dashboard, I felt about as sanguine as any human could feel. Once the orange orb sank down, leaving a silk mango drape across the sky, Cruz fired up the ignition, and off we went in search of bodily nourishment now that our souls had been fed!

Serina, my friend from Laos, who owned the restaurant I chose, greeted us at the door with a hug for both of us. When she was embracing Cruz, she gave me the "wide eye," indicating she approved of my new friend.

We sat in a comfortable booth along the back wall and ordered a variety of dishes, from appetizers to entrees. Serina's daughter brought over a pot of tea that she had begun to brew the minute she saw me enter. I am always amazed at the hospitality southeast Asian people show their guests—there is such grace about them.

Over tea, Cruz began telling me about his day and focused on his meeting with Franky. I listened intently, as I tend to do when I am story-building. I set the scene as he talked and envisioned Franky and Fredo as young teens morphing into grown men. This process of mine was always compelling and expanded my ability to see many sides of a situation.

Cruz said, "Franky paints a picture that's hard to imagine as not true. Fredo's movement and actions *do* seem to fit the profile I have been building. But what I really need now is the one clue linking Fredo to Darlene's final hours. I mean, my gut is leading in this direction, but to move Fredo from "person of interest" to "suspect" is something I am not able to do . . . *yet.*"

Once we had hashed out all the possibilities of Fredo's involvement, I switched gears and brought up the subject of Gus Papadopulos. Cruz listened carefully to every detail that I had learned from Jhana with an on-point curiosity. After one exchange, he even flipped his black book out and scribbled a few notes.

"Paris, you've been involved in investigative reporting. Do you know how I approach interrogation? First, you catch a stone crab in your net. You get him home and put him at ease in a pot of water. Then you turn up the gas a little bit, and he starts to feel a little cozier in water that is more like the temperature of the Gulf waters, *but* you never, ever tell him that you plan to boil him alive because he'll jump out."

Promising me he would do some further digging, I was satisfied—not only sated by the fabulous meal but also by the fineness and fluidity of our conversation. We left the restaurant with a goody bag gifted by my friend with lots of extras and set off for my house.

Both exhausted after a long day, I locked up for the eve-ning, and we headed down the hall toward my room. To say there was magic in the air was an understatement. If there was sorcery going on, then I would be the first to admit to being bewitched!

Chapter 39

Cruz was finding it harder and harder to peel himself out of bed if Paris were beside him when he woke. This second chance at love was something he never expected. *Serendipitous,* some call it. He forced himself out of bed and dressed quietly. He smiled and gazed at his sleeping beauty; he reached down and pulled up the rumpled sheet with a wistful memory of the night before still fresh in his mind.

Cruz had driven off-island and across the causeway before he passed the first car. *Nice,* he thought. *These early dawn hours are like a jewel. Once the beachgoers awaken, the bridge will be backed up to the Trail.* He made the short trip downtown in record time and headed up the elevator to his condo for a quick shower and change.

After showering, checking his mail, and watering the plants, Cruz headed out to the station. Ever since he'd been assigned to this case, he had been speculating about the idea of a boat being involved in Darlene's death. Sand Dollar Island, where Darlene's body had been discovered, was a mere sandbar that rose and retreated from the Pass waters almost daily, depending on the tides. *How did Darlene get there?* It had to have been by boat, he deduced.

At his desk, he began his analytical process. He treated most of his cases in the same manner—by establishing a time-line with a start and an end, and then connecting the dots in between. As the pieces of his puzzle began to take shape, he decided to return to the Yacht Club grounds, where he was hoping to find missing clues. He needed to connect the dots between the time Darlene and Fredo exited through the side door of the Gala and when Fredo returned the limo to his business five hours later.

Cruz headed across the John Ringling Bridge under a gray sky. Although rain can be expected anytime in Sarasota during hurricane season, no storms had been predicted by the Weather Bureau. The grounds and the marina were Cruz's focus on this visit. He parked his sedan in the marina lot and began to survey the environment. *Not too many boaters this morning.* The gray skies were most likely what was keeping the fair-weather sailors away.

He spotted Paul down by the gas dock, speaking to what appeared to be a vendor. Cruz decided he would start at the west end of the marina and work his way around to the end where the gas dock was located. The sparse activity slowed his stroll, all the while compelling his aptitude for mental notation.

He found the locked-gate entrance to Dock C-2 on the west end. This wharf was directly adjacent to the side doors of the ballroom from which Darlene and Fredo exited that fateful evening. As he walked down the ramp to Dock C-2, he observed a line of boat-club rental watercrafts ranging from day cruisers to pontoon boats. The very last pontoon boat on the end had a floppy, oversized cover tied over its sagging canopy and interior, indicating it was out of commission for rentals.

Cruz followed the finger pier down to the end, visually inspecting all of the boats. From all appearances, the rental operation seemed concise and well-operated, the boats in the fleet well-maintained and clean. Cruz then moved onto the next finger pier, which stretched out into the inlet, in order to grab deeper drafts, because the crafts moored in this area were larger power yachts.

Cruz took his time with this dock. From what he knew of Darlene, she was a social climber, and yachts of this caliber would be the kind of styling and profiling she might favor. Toward the end of the dock, in a row set aside for the *big boys,* Cruz spotted a mate and someone he presumed was the yacht's owner, sitting on the aft deck of the vessel named *Indiscretion.* Cruz nodded, smiled in their direction, and called out,

"Say, fellas, how long is she—about 100 feet?"

"You're short by about ten feet, my friend," was the owner's reply.

Cruz quickly quipped, "Nothing indiscreet about that!" which brought a chuckle to all.

The ice broken with Cruz's retort, the ship's owner struck up a brief conversation and then invited the detective to come aboard. Cruz, having never been aboard a private yacht of such scope, readily agreed, climbed up the stationary steps, and stepped down onto the deck, where he was met by the first mate, who led the way to the aft deck.

Cruz shook hands with the owner, who identified himself as James O'Hart and then offered Cruz a seat. After Cruz and Jim O'Hart dispensed with the typical chatter that accompanies an initial meet-and-greet, Cruz led the conversation around to his purpose for the day.

"Jim, what brings me to the marina today is that I've been working on a case involving the death of Darlene D'Angelico; did you know who she was?"

Cruz held his phone out, showing Jim the photo of Darlene.

Jim was quick to reply, "Sure, I knew Darlene, but not well. I have lived in Sarasota since I was thirteen. My mother and I moved here from St. Pete when she divorced my father. I attended the Out of Door Academy and then moved on to Stanford upon graduation. In California, I made the grades but dropped out in my senior year to take up with two buddies in a startup venture-capital firm. When that took off, I sold out, and here I am, enjoying life to the fullest.

"Now, about Darlene. I first met her at a charity function that we held aboard *Indiscretion* several years back. A gorgeous woman—if you go for the enhanced models. As for me, I prefer a little more refinement in my paramours. I found Darlene's company to be charming and well-informed, yet her lusty, emphatic approach to members of the opposite sex, well . . . you get the picture. To me, it was always a huge turnoff. Over the years, we've brushed elbows, but I really can't say I 'knew' her."

Cruz continued, "Do you live on-board your vessel, Jim? I just wondered if you might have been aboard the night Darlene was last seen."

Jim replied, "I do live on-board, but I am not always at this port. I have a full crew that accompanies me to whatever port of call I have lined up. But we were moored here in early August this year, as I was attending the Argyle Gala hosted at the Yacht Club. I know what your next question will be: 'Did I see Darlene at the Gala?' Yes, I did. She was on the arm of someone I didn't recognize, but we did make contact and exchanged pleasantries of a sort."

Cruz was digesting all this information. "Did you notice anything different in her demeanor that night? Did she introduce her date to you when you shook hands?"

Here, O'Hart was definitive in his answer: "No, she didn't—and, even though that was a little strange, I didn't give it much thought. For no other reason, I dismissed it as if she thought of him as dispensable, or that's the feeling I got."

Interesting, Cruz thought, and then continued, "What time did you return to your vessel, Jim?"

"A little after eleven—the speeches were wrapping up, and folks were milling out, so I invited two couples aboard for a nightcap. We were all probably out here on the deck until a little after 1 a.m.," Jim answered.

Cruz was cautious with his next question.

"I'm sure that, with all the activity of folks heading out of the Gala, there was a lot of distraction, but do you remember seeing any boats heading out toward the Intercoastal that night?"

O'Hart replied, "Sorry, Detective. Can't say that I do. Most nights, this marina is quiet, as it hosts Yacht Club members and reciprocal club guests. When you serve that kind of clientele, parties and noise are kept to a minimum."

"I understand," Cruz said as he rose to leave. "Thank you for the invitation to board, Jim. *Indiscretion* is certainly an elegant gal."

Jim smiled a huge grin and quipped, "She gives me no back talk, and she goes wherever I want to go!"

Both gentlemen laughed as Cruz made his way toward the bow, waving at the mate who was now up on the bridge, tending to the electronics.

The next pier down was situated in deep water, as it hosted sailing vessels. Cruz gingerly made his way down this dock, not finding anything of real interest. He spoke with a day sailor who worked downtown as an attorney, but he did not know Darlene or recognize her photo. Cruz's last stroll was at the gas-dock pier at the far east end of the marina. Paul was in the shack at the end and greeted Cruz like an old friend.

"Hey, Detective. You still chasing that skirt?"

Cruz dismissed his brash comment and smiled back at Paul, delivering his own inquiry.

"Say, Paul. The case is still open, and in my line of work, I dig for well-dressed lies in hopes of what they will uncover. You got anything new for me?"

But again, Paul knew little. He'd been off work and off-premises before the Gala ended that evening. This lead was a dead end, and, so, Cruz thought it was time for a new angle.

ChapteR 40

Paris

THE WEEK PASSED QUICKLY, and it was Friday evening already. The Fun Friday Night Book Club was scheduled for its monthly meeting. I had planned a simple menu of tacos with guacamole and chips. To make the conversation flow, I mixed up a batch of margaritas—hey, all my attendees arrive on foot, after all!

Cruz had had his bird-dog nose to the ground all this week. The case of Darlene's death was seemingly consuming him, yet it didn't deter his attentiveness in connecting with me. I treasured that aspect. I remembered how absorbed Harry would get in his cases; he would become almost frenetic when he was chasing a perp. But Cruz's energy was much different. He approached his work—and his life, for that matter—with a calm intelligence. It's funny how both of my serious lovers turned out to be police; it's strange that the two relationships felt so different.

Suzy Atwater was first to arrive that evening. She was carrying her book and notebook in a woven tote, and a bouquet of flowers was in her other hand.

"To brighten your day, although you really don't need them; you're glowing already. . . ." she said. Ignoring the analogy, I thanked her for the arrangement and turned around, looking for a vase. Next thing I knew, Bobbi St. John came sweeping through the door in a brightly colored gauze skirt and white shirt, looking more like a coed than a forty-something woman! The two gals busied themselves arranging the refreshments while I tended to the platters of food.

I'd originally formed this book club with the intention of becoming part of the island community. As it turned out, the gals of Gardenia Lane were the ones who kept it consistent, and so it became a Fun Friday Night Book Club, the bonus part being laughter that was always in generous supply. The lawyers from across the street were in residence and were the last to arrive. They were both wine connoisseurs, so they brought their own beverage, a nice vintage cabernet.

The shrimp and vegetable tacos were a hit. We all ate like ravenous wolves, sitting around the dining table passing bowls and reaching for more napkins. The topic of the latest book we had elected to read was hashed out, and then the conversation moved on to the lawyers' thoughts on the November elections for the County Commission. Once that subject was finished, sneaky Suzy Atwater spoke out about her early-morning observations and detecting a pattern of a handsome certain someone leaving my bungalow in the wee hours.

Bobbi began to giggle, as she always did; as sexually alluring as Bobbi was, she was somewhat of a prude when it came to suggestive conversation. Bemused, I hushed Suzy and artfully changed the subject to Darlene. I related the story of Nico's friend, Gus, starting with my conversation with Taylor Greene, who had first spotted Gus on the island without Nico.

Then I blew the story out full blast and revealed that my source had provided me some details that confirmed that Gus was in Florida. I allowed my suspicions to paint an outrageous plot of Gus taking up with Darlene behind Nico's back and then killing her because she was going to tell his wife and Nico about them!

This conversation resulted in many scenarios being bantered around the table on Gus's possible involvement with Darlene, and my hypothesis drew a lot of guffaws by the time we were done! The lawyers said in unison, "Paris, what an imagination you have!"

The evening was another book-club success, and it broke up around 10:30 p.m. Bobbi stayed behind and helped me put everything away.

"Hey, Paris. You know how you were talking about Nico's friend, Gus? Well, Gus is a friend of mine, too," she said demurely.

Not sure where Bobbi was headed with this revelation, I listened while she continued.

"You know I'm not a kiss-and-tell kinda girl, and I am certainly a grown woman and can make my own choices. Maybe it was a selfish choice, but listen: I ran into Gus earlier this summer in New York. You remember when I went on that promo tour for *Supergirl?* Well, the network always put me up at the Marriott East Side in midtown and, as fate would have it, Gus was staying there, too. One evening in the bar together led to another, and before I knew it, Gus finished up his business and flew down here—and we holed up over a long, rainy weekend."

Holy smokes, I thought, *I didn't expect to be party to a skyhook alibi like that.*

I rallied with a comeback and said, "Listen, Bobbi girl. Your business is your business. I am sorry I was somewhat crass in suggesting Gus would be a suspect in Darlene's murder; that must have hurt your feelings."

Bobbi smiled up at me, rose out of her chair, and gave me a hug. "You know, Paris, I don't form many attachments, but you . . . well, if I had a best friend, I would want her to be just like you . . . *discreet.*"

We ended the evening on that note, and it was a sweet note to end on. I will say, however, I wasn't altogether ready to deep-six my Gus theory, as I really *was* beginning to think he was the one who'd sacked Darlene. I guess the only crime Gus was guilty of was "sacking" my other neighbor!

Chapter 41

Amsterdam, The Netherlands

SEPTEMBER 25

AN ENDLESS SPELL OF RAIN was falling and provided a shroud, camouflaging the man seated indoors at Café Thijssen. From all appearances, he was just a tourist taking respite while waiting for the weather to subside. But actually, he was escaping the friendless life that now surrounded him. His houseboat, moored up to the canal a few hundred yards away, would be a dream for many a young man, but not him—his broken heart wouldn't allow it. It was soaked in overwhelming sorrow. If only she could have loved him the way he loved her, this whole nightmare would never had happened. It would have been so easy had she just said "Yes."

Chapter 42

Paris

THE WEEKEND FLEW BY WITHOUT A HITCH. Cruz's hours were spent in chasing his case and in driving his daughter, Brookelyn, to her soccer commitments, so we had spent very little time together. Monday night had typically become the evening we would reconvene, and I was looking forward to seeing him more than I ever imagined possible.

I spent the morning working on assignments that were due and did some research for my upcoming project for *Vanity Fair* that I was very excited about. It was a feather in my cap to have been chosen to write an article for this important literary magazine. I was glad the editors provided me enough lead time to prepare, because if I hit this plum assignment out of the park, it could lead to more work from that iconic periodical.

Cruz called around four in the afternoon, and we planned to meet at 5:30 p.m. I thought that, since I had been sequestered most of the day, I would enjoy getting out of the house. To change things up a bit, I elected for us to drive over to St. Angelo Square, located on the next Key north, where we could park, walk around, and shop, and then dine at one of the many gourmet restaurants around the piazza. When Cruz arrived (*on time*—another thing I adored about him), we set off in his Jeep and meandered through midtown traffic and across the causeway, which landed us right on St. Angelo Square. We began to hunt for on-street parking and got lucky. On the second artery of the square, we spotted a good-sized SUV pulling out of a prime spot that Cruz was able to snag.

We walked around the square in a nicely syncopated rhythm, mostly window shopping, but we did enter one store that had a beautiful window display featuring a black-and-white midi-dress that was just my style. Cruz encouraged me to try it on, so I did and had the saleslady wrap it up for me, just because Cruz said I looked beautiful in it.

We found a pretty restaurant on the next artery, with an inviting outside dining area bedecked with twinkle lights. After perusing the menu board posted on the sidewalk, we put in our name for our preference of outdoor seating. Once seated, our conversation ran non-stop as we caught each other up on the activities we'd been involved in over the past few days.

I began with the Fun Friday Night Book Club meeting and how it took a turn into an eye-opening surprise with Bobbi

St. John's confession. Although Cruz was visibly surprised by my recount of Bobbi's declaration, he commented that he had a feeling that Gus couldn't be the guy involved with Darlene. He relied heavily on his instincts, and they were not leading him in Gus's direction.

Then our conversation moved on to his investigation and the strides he had made over the weekend. Cruz told me he was moving in on Fredo as a prime suspect but needed to tighten his timeline to detail the hours leading up to the time of death. Interestingly enough, St. Angelo's Square was within a mile of the Bird Bay Yacht Club, so Cruz suggested we take an evening walk through the marina grounds on our way back to St. Michael's Key. That sounded like an exciting prospect to me. I loved following along in his investigation, even if I was just a somewhat-passive observer.

We left the restaurant after the sun had set and headed back to the Jeep. After settling into his seat, Cruz turned to me and put his hand to my cheek, brushing my hair aside. He said,

"Paris, I love you. I love everything about you. But what I love most is the way you make me feel about myself."

Love! Did he just drop the "L" bomb? Wow! This declaration was the first such admission of his having feelings for me. I mean, his language and actions so far had been very clear that we were moving in this direction, but to admit it to me so soon was breaking my heart wide open. I blushed as I replied,

"Cruz, you never cease to amaze me. I'm certainly feeling the same way, but are we moving too quickly?"

As a response to which, he pulled me over and deeply kissed me, leaving me with no doubts.

"No," he spoke in a whisper as I came up for a breath. "Not quickly enough."

And just like that, we were a committed couple, ready to take on the world—or at least to take on solving the elusive case that had brought us together!

Chapter 43

CRUZ AND PARIS REACHED THE YACHT CLUB around 8:30 p.m. and headed down to the dock area. For all intents and purposes, they appeared to be a young couple merely on a stroll. First, they walked down the finger piers, where the power yachts and super yachts were moored. The bulkhead, where *Indiscretion* had been anchored the night Cruz met James O'Hart, was now empty. Cruz surmised that she must be out to sea on another adventure but delighted in recounting to Paris the story of being welcomed aboard such a magnificent yacht. Ambling along, Cruz was making mental notes, while Paris chattered about. When they reached Dock C-2, where the Boat Club Rentals were moored, Cruz noted the pontoon boat with the broken canopy, still in the same position as he had observed it before.

"That's strange," he mused. "Why wouldn't the vessel be repaired and put back into the fleet by now?"

As we started down the wharf where the gas dock was located, the distinctive smell of marijuana was heavy in the air. Cruz and Paris turned to each other and began to giggle as they walked on by. Next, they circled the building, walking around the pool area and taking the path to the dockmaster's office.

Once back in the parking lot, Paris's teeming good mood was apparent. No wonder—she was a girl falling in love. Her thoughts were filled with hope and joy. *He said he loves me!* Paris thought gleefully as they walked along. *Yes, indeed, this one must have been heaven-sent.*

Chapter 44

THE CASE WAS SMOLDERING in Cruz's psyche from the moment he awoke the next morning. Paris was up already and making coffee, a to-go cup of which Cruz requested, explaining that he needed to fly to the station and dive back into his investigation. Since Paris was familiar with this kind of hunger-driven quest, she quickly fixed his cup and hurried him out the door—with a burning kiss to carry him through the day.

Cruz arrived at the station and got to work. He added in notes to his timeline and studied the board. His thoughts were drawing him back to the Yacht Club. He had to return and see if he could unearth anything about a boat going out that fateful night.

He arrived back at the Club around 11:30—there was quite a bit of activity for a Tuesday morning, but the weather conditions were light and breezy, particularly favorable for a day sail. Cruz parked the car in a shady spot on the marina side of the lot and sat inside, with the AC running while observing. He noted there was a new Dockmaster that day with whom he had not yet talked, and, so, he turned off the ignition and headed down to the dock, hoping to intersect the gent. Upon reaching the dock, the dockmaster turned his attention to Cruz and inquired if he could be of assistance. Cruz flashed his badge and explained his business.

"The name is 'Detective Cruz,' sir. With whom do I have the pleasure of speaking?"

The man identified himself as "Tony" and reiterated his working position as dockmaster. With pleasantries set aside, Cruz began his questioning in interview mode, focusing on the known date of death. Cruz showed Darlene's photograph to Tony, who, in turn, gave every indication that he did not recognize her.

Next, Cruz began an inquiry into the rental boats and how they were handled. Tony responded with a concise explanation of the process as to how the fleet was reserved for cruises. Cruz asked if they had a manifest of boats reserved for hire on August 10th.

Tony excused himself and turned to enter the dock shack to retrieve the logbook.

Cruz leafed through the entries but didn't find anything of use. However, he noted that there were entries for eleven watercrafts in the fleet, yet Cruz had counted twelve, including the vessel with the broken canopy. He brought that observation up to Tony, and Tony explained that the craft was not actually part of the fleet but was privately owned and allowed to be moored in the end slot by arrangement with Paul.

Tony went on to say that it was his understanding that the pontoon-style vessel was used as a water taxi and sometimes for sunset sails for clients of the owner of the vessel.

With that sweet tidbit of information, Cruz requested to board the pontoon. Once on-board, he jotted down the vessel's State of Florida ID in his black book before he began his "look around."

His first movement took him toward the broken Bimini canopy top. He carefully lifted the canopy and noted the missing piece, but, in his search around the rest of the deck, he was unable to locate the absent fitting. Next, Cruz directed his movements to the other side of the canopy, the side that was still intact. He carefully lifted the canvas and pushed up the sleeve placket that covered the frame to expose the corresponding piece that was missing from the sagging side. Carefully, he removed the pole and immediately noted the striations of the screw end consistent with the medical examiner's findings. Cruz reached into his pocket and removed a long poly evidence bag and labeled it as he inserted the pipe inside.

Encouraged by this discovery, Cruz moved about the vessel in search of anything else that might look amiss. Keeping his focus tight, he took his time, like the seasoned investigator he was, meticulously covering every inch of the vessel. He always found it useful at this stage of an investigation to slow-walk it, because evidence can have a way of popping out, almost taking on a life of its own.

Unfortunately, time and tide had taken their toll, and if this was the pontoon that Darlene and Fredo were on that fateful night, any evidence of foul play that may have occurred had either been rendered dissipated by weather or was painstakingly wiped devoid of trace elements. Still, Cruz concluded that he needed to disperse his investigative team so that they could do a deep dive.

Cruz spent another hour on-board making copious notes in his black book before he disembarked and headed back to his car. He had a lot of ground to cover. As he bid adieu to the dockmaster, ideas swarmed in his head. He was certain he was about to join the connecting thread, but the absence of a murder weapon left him still in limbo. But, ever the optimist, he thought, *If the threadwork of the corresponding canopy part is a match with the threadwork marks on Darlene's corpse, I may be in a position to draw some major conclusions.*

Chapter 45

FROM THE CAR, CRUZ PUT A CALL IN to the station a little
after two that afternoon. He was flushed with the kind of
provocative incentive that is felt when one is close to crack-
ing a case. He followed up on his thoughts and quickly made
arrangements with the Crime Scene Investigation Unit to
make a sweep of the vessel. The team reached the vessel and
met Cruz shortly after four o'clock.

The dock was rife with cruisers readying their crafts for a
sunset cruise. Just as he had planned, Cruz cordoned off the
vessel with crime-scene tape, a sight that was garnering some
special attention from those cruisers passing by. Once the unit
of three investigators had boarded the boat, the choreographed
and concentrated probe began in earnest. A couple of hours
passed before they concluded their findings and bagged their
evidence. Cruz was always fascinated by the work of the

crime-investigation unit. The process of forensics study, in particular, always provided key elements in connecting the dots toward an eventual solution of the case.

The team and Cruz packed up at the same time, and all headed back to the station, where the analysis of the data collected would be immediately undertaken. Most interesting to Cruz was the scant trace of blood found in a ridge of the patterned deck of the boat. Faded by time from red to murky brown, it was mostly undetectable to the naked eye, but once discovered and carefully lifted, and, although dried and aged, it could still prove to be sufficient to provide a DNA match, either to the victim or the suspect.

Chapter 46

ONCE BACK AT THE STATION, Cruz placed a call to Paris. In their haste to get underway on this morning, they had not had the opportunity to make any plans. Paris picked up on the first ring and, with her singsong voice, calmed Cruz's anxiety simply with her lilting tone.

"Hey, boyfriend," Paris cooed. "How goes the grind?"

Flush with information, Cruz spilled out a torrent of facts that he had uncovered, which left him breathless.

"This is fascinating, Cruz; your hunches are really paying off. Is there anything I can do for you or help you with?"

"No, baby. I'm good. I'm going to grab something to eat and make it a night here at the station while we put some pieces together. What will you do with your time tonight?"

Paris thought for a minute and said, "I think I'll call it an early night myself. I've been at the computer all day, which has left me with a stiff neck. Also, Brookelyn asked for my help in researching anthropoids for a report she's been working on, so, of course, I supplied her with a mountain of data and ideas!"

That sentiment further warmed Cruz's heart. It was hard to believe that, in the very short time since meeting Paris, their relationship had blossomed into what was becoming a full-fledged romance.

When their conversation had covered all the topics at hand, Cruz hung up with a promise to call in the morning and check in.

"Wish me luck, baby."

"*Luck*, Cruz? Why, you don't believe in things as mercurial as that, do you? I'll wish you fruition—yes, *that's* what I'll send you off with—that your efforts will bear you fruits!"

Cruz smiled through the receiver, thinking to himself, *God Almighty, I love the way that girl thinks!*

Chapter 47

T HE "SMOKING GUN" WAS FINALLY UNCOVERED. The DNA
match from the dried-blood sample proved the blood was
Darlene's. Also, the vessel ID that Cruz had sent off to the
Fish and Wildlife Administration showed the pontoon boat to
be registered to an "Alfredo Cordone" and listed the address
of Elite Town Car Service. Fredo, it seemed, had a little side
hustle that Franky wasn't really aware of. Innocent as that
may have appeared, in this case, his side hustle was anything
but free from wrongdoing. Although Cruz was not sure of
the motive for such a crime, he was certain that Fredo had
killed Darlene.

Cruz slacked back in his desk chair and breathed a sigh
of accomplishment. He was zeroing in on a solution, but he

had to cross all the proverbial t's, dot the i's, make arrangements to meet Fredo's return flight, due in tomorrow night, and promptly place him under arrest for the murder of Darlene D'Angelico!

Chapter 48

THE SCENE WAS SET at the Sarasota Bradenton International Airport the night of September 30th. Cruz was present, along with two uniformed officers. The Southwest flight showed up on time, and the trio lay in wait. Passengers began to emerge from the jetway shortly after 10:15 p.m., but, as the procession dwindled, there was no Fredo. Immediately, Cruz contacted the airlines to check the manifest. Although it showed that Alfredo Cordone was scheduled to take the flight, he had failed to check in prior to departure and, therefore, was not on the flight's roster; the flight had departed one soul short.

Chapter 49

Amsterdam, The Netherlands

THE AFTERNOON RAIN in the Canal District had subsided—almost stopping—as pedestrian life began to fully resume amid the drippy conditions. Yet, the boat docked nearest to the *Magere Brug*, the skinny bridge crossing the Amstel, was quiet. The gentle rocking of the boat had lulled its owner, casting him into another restless sleep filled with haunting dreams—as if he were reliving the horror after horror of a destroyed life in his sleep. This dream was pervasive—the images repeated from start to finish, recounting each turn of events from the night his life had turned from sweet anticipation to complete disaster.

His frenzied sleep would vacillate between dream and stark reality, with flashing visions that he desperately hoped to be rewritten with a new ending, but every gruesome detail inevitably led him to the same, dismal conclusion. Fredo could "feel" the nighttime air fresh on his face as he and Darlene stepped out of the stuffy ballroom that night. He could hear her voice as clear as day as she exclaimed,

"Fredo, catching the fireworks over the water is a great idea."

Fredo, setting the tone by protectively draping his hand over Darlene's shoulder, said, "You're a blast, doll—this is going to be fun. Remove your shoes. It will make it easier to navigate the pier."

Darlene, reacting as though this overture was absurd, nevertheless heeded the call by slipping off her Christian Louboutins and tucking them under her arm; then she allowed Fredo to lead her down to Dock C-2.

Fredo's dreams were such that he could actually "hear" the speeches droning on off in the distance as the two stepped aboard a waiting pontoon boat. The boat was just as Fredo had outfitted it—stocked and ready for his planned evening cruise.

Sweat emanating from his pores and a racing heart invaded Fredo's dream as it played on in his head—as if he were a distant bystander. He cast off the lines and stepped behind the helm, maneuvering his way out of the canal and heading for the open waters of Roberts Bay.

The vision of Darlene enjoying the night air and letting her walls down for a change allowed Fredo to see her youth emerge as she tied her meticulously tinted hair back with an Hermès scarf, fitting it around her head and neck in true Italian fashion. She was poised and seated up toward the bow, her perfectly pedicured bare feet tucked beneath her. The thin moonlight barely showed the fine-line facial wrinkles that she was always so desperate to hide. Out on the open Bay, Fredo was heading for the Pass and Samson Beach—the perfect vantage point from which to delight Darlene with a fireworks display—and a fiery proposal.

As the dream continued, Fredo watched it all unfold again, just as if it were in real time. The combination of the casual manner he took in dropping the anchor, along with the way the two eventually settled on the aft-deck bench seat, was affording him an altered state of reality. The choreographed dance that Fredo was anticipating in getting Darlene into a receptive state of mind was nothing short of perfection. A flute of champagne and some intoxicating music all augmented this dream sequence.

His efforts paid off in his dream, just as they had in reality, yet Darlene's shift in attitude as she began to get a whiff of something amiss was apparent. This was one segment Fredo could not change in his dreams. The haunting memory of the evening's dialogue, especially that phrase ". . . being on the water is always so calming" that Darlene offered was thrilling Fredo to no end, as if she were ultimately, if reluctantly, surrendering to the moment.

Fredo's dream thoughts opened a seemingly easy—at least to him—path, for what he was contemplating as an avowal that could fulfill his lifelong desire.

"Darlene, I've been thinking. It's been almost twenty years since the first time I drove you up in New Jersey. Hell, it was my first job—driving for the dock bosses. I was just a kid, really; and you . . . you were this eighteen-year-old girl, wild and tame at the same time, married to that Calisto fellow—"Cal," right? Well, I knew you were a doll married to a heavy hitter of a husband and with a big sparkler on your hand, so there was no room for dreaming that dream, but honest to God, Darlene, it was back then that I fell for you. I couldn't help it. You stood out like a goddess. The dock bosses laughed at my puppy-love crush, but, try as I might, I never got the vision of you outta my system."

As Fredo continued his self-absorbed, dewy maunderings, Darlene sat stonily staring at the night sky, like some astronomer scouring the heavens for constellations, her icy body language clearly demonstrating her mounting annoyance. Even in his dream, the dialogue could not be changed:

"So, it had to be kismet, Darlene, that you surfaced down here on the exact island as me and as single as I am."

Again, Darlene was silent. Seething, but silent. Before she could object, Fredo continued,

"The way we reconnected several years back—you coming out of Marina John's and me dropping off a fare, we were destined. You called to me: 'Hey, I remember you. What's your name?' That was it; then you said, 'I want you to be my driver from now on.'"

Fredo began to thrash in his sleep as the nightmare raced forward toward the climax. Darlene broke his ridiculous dialogue by saying, "Fredo, hey. I mean this is all nice and all, but really, are you professing love or something for me? Because, really, I mean you can't honestly believe I could . . ."

Fredo was panicking but still pressing on with, "I am serious, Darlene. Listen, remember when you were a young bride, and I had to pick you and Mr. Calisto up at the airport?"

"Yes," Darlene answered. "What about it?"

"Well, you know how Calisto was set to make a stop and you were told to stay in the car with me? That night, you were so happy and chattering away. You had just come from business in Sicily, and you told me all about a side trip Cal took you on to Amsterdam. You talked about how enchanted you were with the city, how free you felt stay-ing aboard a houseboat moored in a charming canal, how you loved the sway of the boat and how it rocked you to sleep. You said it was the very best time of your life. Do you remember that?"

Fredo looked over at Darlene and caught her faint smile. She remembered.

"Of course, I could never forget that trip—it was like rapture. To be young and in love with a powerful man in a magical place—yes, those are moments one never forgets."

Fredo, excited and thinking he that he was making strides, bore on. "Well, Darlene, I'm going to give you back that mesmerizing memory. I've bought us a houseboat, and it's waiting for us along the Prinsengracht in Amsterdam. I've been stashing money from a few extracurriculars, and we've got enough. I want to marry you, Darlene. I love you. I am crazy about every inch of you. We will live your happy dream for the rest of our lives."

That's when the dream split apart the silence, with the sound of heinous laughter coming from Darlene's twisted mouth. "Fredo, you *might* just be out of your mind. You are delusional and talking like a mad person. Clearly, you know, I am not in your league—there is no way I would ever lower myself to your level. I mean, do you know who I am? Where I've been? Who I know? How could you . . . you a simple servant, a driver without even a touch of class, ever think you could have someone like me?"

Her laugh echoed down into the chambers of Fredo's heart, as his rage bubbled up. He stood up, rocking the boat, and steadied himself by grabbing the Bimini top, his strength knocking the frame out of its socket and the end coming off in his hand as Darlene continued,

"You are no more than a Hoboken hick. You are nothing. Fredo, you come from nothing; you're a nobody."

"Don't say that, Darlene—just listen . . . digest the idea for a minute. Come on, doll—give it a chance. . . ."

It was the mocking sarcasm and the piercing scoff Fredo heard her emit next that drove the insanity. In the dream, as in reality, came the angry cry of an animal, a growl, almost, as Fredo wielded the pipe end of the Bimini frame, hitting Darlene so hard that she fell to the deck. He came down on her head again and again, bashing it until her body fell silent. The horror of the dream's scene detailed his fueled rage, as he heaved her body over the side of the boat with the strength of a longshoreman, into the shallow water off Samson Beach, like he was cleansing himself of a scourge.

As his nightmare metamorphosed between dream and consciousness, it finally neared a conclusion. Fredo could "see" the sequence of him frantically pulling up the anchor, starting the engine and heading back to the Yacht Club, where he and Darlene had begun the night's events. As the dream dwindled toward the end, the scene was brought to a close, and Fredo headed to the open waters of the Bay, leaving behind all evidence of Darlene, whom he had just dumped for shark food.

On that misty afternoon in Amsterdam, Fredo began to roust from his frightful recount of this sordid nightmare. The peace and tranquility he sought would never be granted to him again.

Epilogue

Cruz was on his way to meet me for a rendezvous up on Little Beach. Traffic was heavy coming onto the island, with folks gathering for the Drum Circle, held every Sunday night down at the main beach, so I planned to walk over and secure a spot for us.

I left my bungalow, knowing Cruz would be along shortly. I reached the beach, set up two chairs, and then walked to the sea's edge. The sun was beginning its descent, but it was still high enough in the sky to provide warmth to my face.

I closed my eyes and gave thanks for the day. So much grace had been bestowed on me over the past two months that I felt immensely mindful of my riches and grateful for every one of them.

As I stood inert, I felt two arms encircle my waist and a tender nuzzle come down on my neck! Cruz had arrived, and joy swept through me like a blinding desire. We remained, slightly swaying, at the water's edge, wearing beautiful smiles for a perfect moment in time before returning to our waiting chairs.

As we sat in repose, Cruz began his tale of how the mystery had unraveled. I listened intently to the full account, wanting to understand the entire plot from start to finish. As Cruz laid out all the threads that led him to his suspect, I was dazzled by his keen perception and the precision of his investigation.

"I may not have been able to actually 'collar' the suspect this time," Cruz explained, "but I did not stop at that dead end. Once I learned Fredo was on the lam, I ran his passport through the system and was able to determine he was hiding out in The Netherlands. Once I had that information, it wasn't difficult to locate his exact whereabouts in Amsterdam. Interpol is now on the case; it's about midnight over there, so, I suspect that, by morning light, Fredo will be apprehended and held under an extradition order to be returned to the United States."

Cruz was almost giddy as he told me the news.

As for me, I was dizzy with the result of everything that had happened. My quiet island was now without the stain of an unsolved murder, and my previously non-existent love life was now filled with an overflowing romance with infinite possibilities. I mean, even though I do not believe in happenstance at all, there was a bit of *Lady Luck* at play here. Of that, I was certain!

THE END

Acknowledgments

THE CHARACTERS OF THIS NOVEL are, naturally, borrowed from my own experiences and are sometimes recognizable by type. Composites of their collective animation in print, however, are difficult to camouflage. All the characters live within me. Otherwise, I could not possibly give them life.

I wish to thank the following folks for their assistance in bringing this story to print.

My eternal gratitude goes to my editor, Danny Ray, for his insightful intelligence. Danny, you have taught me how to expand my prose and how to withhold it to build to a crescendo. By poking holes in all the right places, you have made me a better writer.

My deep appreciation goes to my marketing partner, Lynn McGinnis. When you put the beginning nine chapters in front of me, you encouraged the birth of the finished story. *Brava, bella!*

I wish to acknowledge the invaluable assistance of Ret. Sheriff Glenn Gaither, Charles County, Maryland, Sheriff's Department, and his lovely wife, Cindy, for providing the lowdown on the inner workings of a homicide investigation. I never realized how zany talking about murder could be!

Throughout this journey, I am reminded that none of my books would ever get completed if not for the devotion and unconditional love of my husband and leader of my tribe, Ron. Your belief in my writing fills my cup. I owe everything to you.

And finally, to my readers, who have read my books and followed my writing over the years, thank you! You are the reason I am propelled to write. Every book I publish is because of you!

About the Author

D.J. POSNER IS A NATIVE OF WASHINGTON, D.C. and now resides on the Gulf coast of Florida surrounded by the alluring islands of Sarasota. Her husband and two furry muses are her source of inspiration and perpetuate a joy-filled spirit within her. By sharing her writing with readers, she hopes to inspire them to find and claim the same peace for themselves.

www.ingramcontent.com/pod-product-compliance
Lightning Source LLC
Chambersburg PA
CBHW060600190726
48283CB00003B/1092